AF472628

SUBCULTURE

Warren Hargodd

All characters in this publication are fictitious

and any resemblance to real persons, living or dead,

is purely coincidental.

ISBN 978-1-4457-0247-6

For Landé and Coco.

SUBCULTURE

I

14.231.724-0

The sunrise continued to spill over the walls and rooftops of the city. Air conditioning units hummed as they inhaled, traffic lights changed colour, pedestrians crossed streets, leaves danced on the branches of trees. U-Bahn trains rattled through tunnels and over viaducts, recorded voices announced stops on the tram system and people watched computer or television screens as they consumed their breakfasts.

Matthias smiled as the waitress set down a second cup of espresso in front of him and scurried off to the next table. She didn't seem to notice, but the sun was still relatively low and she may have mistaken the expression for grimacing in the morning light. Using the handle of his spoon, he prodded the small complimentary biscuit around the edge of the saucer, while Thomas continued rattling off his questions, as the miniature spools of tape rotated in his dictation machine between them on the table.

"I think it's a wonderful setting for a story," he went on, "but what about the actual plot?"

"Hmm?"

"It's full of—excuse me." He covered his mouth and made a cough with a *hargh* sound. "Sorry. …subtle commentary on everything that's happening right now, here on Earth. Global warming, the war in the middle east, all retold allegorically, as space opera. I think, if you sat down and wrote all that out as a novel or a script for a sci-fi movie, you'd make a fortune. It's just that there's no real plot. Where's the man caught in the middle of it all, fighting to change things for the better, getting the girl, all that human interest stuff? Or *alien interest*, I should say."

Matthias blinked at him a few times as he tried to comprehend the meaning of this latest query. Everything he'd asked so far had been straight-forward stuff about politics, technology, the mechanics that made a stellar empire tick. This last track threw him a bit.

At the table next to them, a man in a business suit picked at a breakfast of sliced fruit and cheese, browsing through a copy of *Der Zeit*. On the front page, the Convention on the Future of Europe was presenting its first draft of the European Constitution to sceptical leaders and England was shocked by the suicide of a government intelligence advisor. Columnists whinged about the hottest summer since records began. The man seemed irritated as he turned the pages, perhaps because of the uneven paving causing his table to wobble and some juice to slop from the glass.

"Alright," Matthias began, slowly. "I suppose I'm not such a good story teller when it comes to the lives of individual characters, but I'll give it a try. We start with one individual who, by human standards, has committed a crime and is no longer welcomed by his people…"

Thomas was a native to Berlin and Matthias had first met him the evening before at a biergarten on Schönhauser Alle. They had chatted for a couple of hours about the world's problems and where Saddam Hussein might be hiding, before the conversation topic had turned to other worlds and how more enlightened cultures might deal with the Earth's issues. The summer night had been warm and hours had seemed to melt away as they sat at a table poring over these ideas. Berlin had a high rate of unemployment which, coupled with the vacationing students and a deluge of tourists, meant there was no shortage of people willing to stay up drinking late. Thomas was in his mid-twenties, had an overly serious-looking square face, framed by wiry light brown hair, and very alert-looking eyes. He worked at an electronics factory, although he also pitched ideas for books and radio plays during his spare time, so far without much success. He became fascinated by Matthias's stories and it wasn't until nearly 4am, after the biergarten had shut its gates and they had relocated to a nearby café bar to continue the conversation, that Thomas decided he had to leave and get a few hours of sleep before his next factory shift. Before leaving, he'd mentioned he always ate breakfast at the same café each morning, and would bring a cassette recorder with him this time, so Matthias was waiting there when he arrived.

"… As I mentioned last night, such an advanced society has no need for a police force or judicial system, but if a member of the culture has violated the accepted order in some harmful way, then I suppose you could say there'd be a strong pressure put on this person to leave."

"So, they'd like excommunicate him?"

"Right. It's not that he'd have social privileges withdrawn, not in a formal sense, but there would be a mutual understanding that he has to take himself away from the society and its normal sphere of influence."

"I take it this utopian society doesn't have a death penalty, then?"

Matthias shifted uncomfortably, involuntarily pinching together the end of his aquiline nose. "I didn't ever describe it as utopian. Perhaps it might be seen that way, judged by the standards of this world…" He looked vague for a moment before continuing. "I think it would be normal in the development of most species, I mean when developing as a civilisation, to pass through a phase where they have successfully addressed the social, political and economic problems of their homeworld, before they are able or perhaps willing to embark on large-scale colonial expansion.

"Some beings, particularly those with swarm or hive mentalities, might achieve this as an escalating process of mutual cooperation, as different societal groups make contact, merge and become super-collectives. Other races might do it more chaotically, often after many generations of war and bloodshed. But sooner or later, as long as they don't wipe themselves out first, I suppose a culture will achieve a state *you'd* call utopia. Of course, that's not the end of the story. Once they've got there, there are a lot of new and often unforeseen challenges to face, so to them the concept of 'utopia' eventually becomes either unattainable or just plain meaningless." He trailed off again and mad the gesture with his nose once more. "I'm rambling. Sorry, I do that."

"I know."

"Well in any case, no, there's not normally a death sentence. Beings in such an advanced state normally would have found ways to greatly extend their natural life spans. If killing someone is a big deal to you people, imagine how much worse it is to cut a being down in his prime when he could have had centuries or millennia of achievements still to come."

"I see. But…" *hargh hargh* "… sorry. But you said 'not normally.' Does that mean there are exceptions?"

"I suppose. The point is, it wouldn't normally be needed."

"If you'd been here in this city sixty years ago, and you saw Adolf Hitler crossing the street, would you have run him down in your car?"

Matthias's frown returned, deeper. "Yes," he admitted. "If I'd been there and I was fully aware of what he was doing, I would have."

There was a moment's silence. Thomas glanced back down at the dictation machine. Matthias followed his gaze, but also noted a balding, ruddy-faced man in an expensive-looking, gaudy striped shirt, who had seated himself a lone two tables away, and was giving them a bit of a funny look. He dismissed this and looked back at the rotating tape reels in their clear plastic shell. Somewhere outside another café nearby, a wandering busker was murdering Supertramp's 'Breakfast in America.'

"So, back to the saga of our alien individual." *hargh* "Our hero's an exile then, trying to clear his name?"

Matthias smiled faintly at Thomas's idea, but also wondering if that really was a cough or some sort of bizarre nervous twitch. He'd been doing it often the previous night as well while they were drinking. "Yeah, why not? Of course, for a culture of this sort of age and technological prowess, the 'sphere of influence' could be a very large region. You remember last night, we imagined how a race which had achieved interstellar travel might claim an uninhabited planetary system and turn it into a huge power plant, converting the star's mass into energy?"

"So to get out from under these people's feet, you'd need to travel a lo-o-o-ong way."

"What do you mean? You said 'you'd need to travel?'"

"Huh?"

Matthias frowned, confused. "'You'd need to—‘‘

"No no, I was talking rhetorically. It's just the way I think, you see, I normally write my fiction in the first person. God, did you think I wanted to write *you* into this as the hero?"

They both laughed.

hargh

"Really, yes, he has to travel a long way to escape their attention. It's not physically feasible to have faster-than-light communication, so some of the remoter settlements might not know about one of these 'social disconnections' for a while, but because in such a society everyone – to some extent - knows everything which everybody else is doing, knowledge will catch up with them eventually and he'll once again have to move on. Just keep going, until he's beyond the boundary of their occupied space. "The galaxy contains vast unoccupied regions where someone could feasibly hide out, maybe set up a small hermit-hole on an asteroid or even begin a little commune for other, similar outcasts. Some might do that."

Thomas leant forward a little. "But our fugitive hero wants to… what? Find other misfits who've been wronged by the system? Raise an army to fight back? Keep running because sinister agents of his own people are in pursuit?"

This last suggestion caused a flicker of amusement to play on Matthias's face. "It sounds like a thriller in the making now."

"Doesn't it just? Needs some more work done yet, though. I mean it, this could be big, but it's got to stand out from the rest of the paperback market. It's all very well to produce something which sits on shelves in airport shops, but—" He snorted. "Why aim for that? Fuck that, there are nobler ambitions to have, you know? This is good quality stuff."

The waitress reappeared from inside the café and Thomas tried in vain to get her attention as she made her way to one of the other outside tables. "Or," he continued, "one other possibility: you're a pariah from a super-evolved alien culture…"

Again, this made Matthias look a little uncomfortable, but this time Thomas was too wrapped up in his idea-spinning to notice.

"You flee across an endless gulf of interstellar space, all on your own, going slowly crazy from isolation in your personal travel capsule, and then what happens?"

Matthias shrugged.

“You pick up radio signals coming from a small backwater” *hargh* “planet which hardly anybody’s heard of,” he paused for effect, spreading his hands wide to indicating the world around them, “and you think, hey, what a perfect place to hide out. You’ve got some political secret which could change everything back home, something really world-shattering, and mercenaries and police from all over the galaxy are on your tail. You find this little, bitty blue planet in the middle of nowhere and hope to blend in there unnoticed – maybe you disguise yourself under a layer of fake skin or something so the natives don’t get suspicious.”

Matthias relaxed his posture a little, but Thomas had noticed his discomfort and looked puzzled. He hushed his voice a little. “I’m sorry. Was I talking loudly?”

“No, no, it’s okay.”

Matthias continued his discourse in a whisper nonetheless, leaning closer to the recorder and compensating for the loss of volume by gesticulating more with his hands. “The authorities here on earth discover there’s an alien living amongst them—“

“How would they do that?” Matthias interjected.

“Uhh –“ Thomas floundered for a moment, his train of thought momentarily derailed. “Well, that doesn’t matter hugely at this stage, it’s not essential to the overall plot. Let’s say…” He paused again to wave at the waitress. This time she saw him and he made a frantic mime of wanting the bill. “Let’s say his craft was tracked by radar. Or he takes off his disguise to recharge himself and somebody sees him do it… yeah, suppose a child witnessed his alien form, but the adults are at first sceptical of the kid’s story… we have subplots building now and everything.”

"I don't know," Matthias sighed, draining the last of his espresso and sitting back on his chair with an affected look of boredom. "I think this might be starting to stray into clichéd territory. And I really think plausible detail is essential to such a story, and would human-built detection systems really be able to spot the arrival of a being whose technological heritage is thousands of years more advanced? And who's to say a being from another star system would be able to blend in seamlessly with humans anyway, just by applying a new layer of skin?"

"It worked for David Bowie, in that film *The Man Who Fell to Earth*." *hargh*

"I haven't seen it."

"Really? You surprise me. But, like I said, how he (or she) gets spotted is not especially relevant at this stage—"

They were both startled by a click from the dictation machine.

"Damn. I didn't bring a spare tape."

The waitress appeared with a bill and the three of them fumbled with loose change. When the coins had finished changing hands and she had departed again, Thomas continued: "Not that we've got time to continue now, anyway. I'm already running late for my shift. And aren't you tired from last night?"

Matthias shrugged. "I'm not much of a sleeper."

"Well anyway, do you want to do this again tomorrow? I feel we're really getting somewhere."

"No, can't, I'm afraid. I have to travel back to Zürich later today, I'm not certain when I'll next be in Germany."

"Oh, what a pity. Well, do you have a handy number or an email address? There's so much more we could discuss."

"How about I take yours? I don't know when I'll next get to sit in front of a computer, but when I do, I'll look you up."

II

14.231.724-2

They parted company hurriedly and Thomas went in the direction of the nearest U-Bahn station, Matthias strolled the opposite way down Kastanienalle, savouring the occasional breaks in the glaring sun which were offered by the chestnut trees. Aside from meeting Thomas at the café – a decision which he now faintly regretted – his day had nothing in the way of an agenda and a dozen possibilities now competed for his attention. He had been in this city for a week, and had already taken one long walk through the middle of its sprawling Tiergarten - where the Kaiser had once hunted game in the days of the German monarchy and hundreds of thousands of bright-haired ravers had now gathered amongst the trees and columns and statues for a noisy open air music festival – and he contemplated exploring some more of this huge green space. Yet it was already a hot, cloudless day, and he would most likely be walking around in the sun for hours.

The modernist concrete needle of the Berlin TV Tower pierced the sky, two hundred metres above the city, and he contemplated waiting for the (air conditioned) observation deck café to open, then sit up there all day, sucking on beer bottles and being regaled by tedious stories from bright eyed tourists from every corner of the Earth. That plan had some appeal, but again, he'd done it once already in the last week.

No, he had to think simpler and found himself stopping off at the nearest grocers to buy a bottle of fizzy drink, then making his way to the much nearer, and smaller, Weinberg civic park. Parents milled around their naked offspring, who played around battered metal water fountains, cast in stark geometric forms – clearly these had seemed like a progressive idea to the planners of the old communist government. Matthias continued past this and into the open green space of the main park. It seemed that anybody who lived within a kilometre of the park and didn't currently need to be anywhere else was jostling for a place to sit in the shade of the trees, while a few brave (or foolish) individuals had stripped off a layer or two and were turning their skin pink in the middle of the open space. At the far end, some punks with beer cans, mohawked hair and sun-defying spiked jackets milled around their dogs, who were playing in green, slimy pond water, in a strange parody of the parents and children.

In the traditional local fashion, he popped the crown from his bottle using the butt of a cigarette lighter, then sat cross-legged on the border of a crowded area of shadow. He watched the fighting dogs in the distance through the lenses of his shades, felt a faint hint of a breeze moving his hair around, breathed in the smell of plant life, sun cream, cigarette smoke and somebody far away trying to get a barbecue started. Far away, children and dogs splashed, a plane droned overhead and somebody was jingling a bicycle bell impatiently.

"Excuse me, can I sit here?"

Matthias snapped out of his daydream, to see a large, bullish figure looming over him, silhouetted in the glare. It took a few moments to register this was the ruddy-faced man who had sat two tables away at the café.

"Uhh, sure," he said, uncertain whether or not to openly question why this man seemed to have followed him.

The man settled himself down in a similarly cross-legged fashion, carefully tucking the edges of his stripy shirt into his trousers. "You are Diagrax, aren't you?" he asked in hushed tones.

Matthias stared back in slack-jawed astonishment. However this man had known, there now seemed little point in trying to deny it. "Yes. And are you?"

"No, I'm not. My name – here – is Bernhard. I have a very strong sense of smell, you see. A Diagrax isn't that hard to locate. Do you mind if I ask why you're in this city?"

Matthias shrugged, unsure of whether Bernhard was accusing him of anything. "No particular reason. Why not? It seemed interesting. Oh, and I'm—"

"Matthias; I caught your name earlier when you were talking to that human."

Matthias began to feel sick in the pit of his stomach. The word 'Diagrax' would be meaningless to anybody else around them listening in, and he was not particularly worried about being outed in this fashion anyway, since people would at worst just assume he was crazy and pretend not to see him. What did bother him was that there was anybody here at all, besides him, who did not belong. Who was now seeking out his company, perhaps to try and befriend him, when he'd come here with the specific purpose of being alone.

"You told him you're from Zürich. Heh, that's pretty funny. Do people here pick up on your accent not being quite right?"

"Wow Bernhard, I must say, when you came over here after me, I thought you were going to chide me for being indiscreet at the café. I guess not."

Bernhard blew a dismissive raspberry. "These people don't care what we talk about. They're too wrapped up in the details of their own lives, especially to be dealing with intrusions in their world they don't know how to deal with. The only people who pay any mind to us are the kind of crank nobody listens to anyway."

"I take it you've been here for a while, then?"

Bernhard nodded. "Actually, that's one of the reasons I need to talk to you. I'm not Diagrax; I think you probably figured that out already."

Matthias nodded.

"I'm a Cephalus."

"Ah. Well, I wouldn't have guessed that! I… I've never actually met a Cephalus, but I gathered you'd be a bit too, well, *big* to fit into a human body?"

"Correct." Bernhard pointed to the centre of his chest with a pudgy finger. "It's just my brain in here. Everything else had to be left behind. I was exiled a while back for… well, I suppose they'd call it manslaughter here. It wasn't my fault- some idiot mis-planned a military exercise, could have happened on anybody's watch, but the bastards needed somebody to scapegoat for it—"

"I hardly think you need to apologise to *me* for being here."

"Quite. Well, I noticed the scent of a newcomer in the city a few days ago, and when I realised where you must be from, I knew I had to come looking."

"I feel so honoured. Okay, Mister Cephalus," as Matthias spoke these words, he remembered that Cephalus are an asexual species, which added some further irony to this encounter, "what exactly is your business here with me?"

Bernhard straightened his posture before getting straight to business. "Your people are known for their prowess with biological and genetic matters. I have a problem in this area and I need your help. If you are prepared to help me, I will locate other members of your kind for you, here on Earth."

"That's an interesting proposal, Bernhard. I must be frank: firstly, what makes you so sure that I can fix your problem? Secondly, what makes you so sure I want to be surrounded by other Diagrax, after I've spent five human lifetimes hurtling through space to get away from them? And lastly, if you've found other Diagrax on this planet – which, frankly, I doubt – then why are you not already employing them instead of me?" Matthias paused, uncertain of how the Cephalus would respond. They were widely considered to be a warlike race, although how that might apply to one individual, separated from his natural form and surrounded by hundreds of potential witnesses was questionable.

Bernhard looked as though he might cry. "They c-couldn't help me," he stammered. "Believe me, I tried everything. You talk about journeys lasting centuries as if that's nothing… to me that would be heavenly. My people are not as forgiving as yours; as my punishment for this *accident* was not only exile here, but to become one of these primitives for as long as I live. Which, considering I've inherited a human lifespan, does not look like being very long."

Matthias swallowed hard and tried to look as detached as possible from this story. He'd hoped to find a way of leaving Bernhard behind, before the man had a chance of plying him with sad tales, but the Cephalus was clearly not going to give up easily, whatever he did.

"I see."

"Look at that human woman there. Look at the way her hair is colourless and thinning, and her face so hollow and cracked. She doesn't have long left. God damn it, she must be barely seventy Earth years old. Seventy-five at a push. Can you imagine that? That's enough time to accomplish *what?*"

"Alright, I see your point."

"You do?"

He let out a deep sigh. It was true, he had in the past been involved in genetic manipulation, although his specialism lay mainly with more mundane problems, and simpler life forms. He knew enough however to know that this problem was theoretically treatable. This really wasn't an affair he wanted to get involved with, especially so soon after arriving on Earth, but this creature's predicament carried an undeniable amount of pathos. He was centuries of travel away from the Cephalus Empire, and it seemed inconceivable that any of his kind would come visiting, to check up on how such a lonely exile was doing. More likely, they'd already forgotten him.

"I can't make any promises. But it could work. I'll need to do some tests."

"You'd do that?"

"Your predicament doesn't leave me much choice. I might have some grievances with my kind, but they didn't tamper with my life expectancy."

"You won't regret this. You know, there's a whole network of our kind here—"

"*Our* kind?"

"'Extraterrestrials'. Ex pats." He giggled at the idea, but it sounded a little laboured to Matthias. "From more than a dozen stars, here in this city. You didn't think you were all alone on this planet, did you?"

Matthias was about to quip "*I should be so lucky*" but checked himself. He could already see where this was going to end up. If Bernhard had the ability to smell him out, then no doubt other would before too long. Whether he was comfortable with the idea or not, he'd end up meeting them.

III

14.231.728-4

Bernhard was a bulky man and he sat awkwardly on the small foam sofa in Matthias's living room. The Earth had been through its day-night cycle twice since their last meeting in the park, but summer rolled on relentlessly and, although the sun was at last setting again, the apartment remained hot and stuffy, even with the window open. An unending hiss of traffic noise poured in from six storeys beneath, broken by occasional horns or sirens. A German-dubbed episode of *Spongebob Squarepants* played on a battered portable TV, barely audible, but Bernhard's eyes flicked back and forth over the screen.

"I can't believe you've lived here for a week and you still don't have curtains up. Doesn't the light bother you?"

"Why would it?" Matthias replied, from the kitchen. "I don't sleep, remember."

"Ah, of course. That, I find pretty strange. I have to sleep. I'm effectively human, and have been for the two and a half decades I've been here. I got used to their whole biorhythm very early on."

"Effectively human?" Enquired the disembodied voice from beyond the door. "The DNA from your body shell's the real deal. After all the time you've lived in that carcass, so much hormonal and genetic gunk's collected in your brain, I'm surprised you can still remember what it feels like to be an off-worlder."

Bernhard shifted uncomfortably on the uneven cushions, turning that thought over in his mind to work out whether or not it was an outright insult. "Well, I do remember," he said at last.

"So tell me," Matthias asked, "when did you actually first get here? Have you always lived on this continent?"

"I was exiled in… god, it's hard to think in Standard Calendar any more. I think it was in 14.221.415. The nineteen-seventies, in the Gregorian system. I didn't settle here straight away; I was in Paris to start off with. Have you been there?"

"No, not yet."

"It's nice. Nicer than Berlin was at the time. The Wall was up, the Earth was in so much political upheaval."

"And it isn't today?"

"Well yes, obviously it is, but it's different now. Then it was all about political ideology. Now it's religious dogma running amuck. Of course, I've stayed as detached from it all as I can; I mean without standing out too much. It's like… have you watched those nature films they have on television here? The ones with lions and cheetahs and things, killing other creatures? You've got to make yourself like the film crew who make these things. You know what I mean?"

"I'm afraid I do. Did you leave your normal form behind, before you travelled?"

"Yeah, my authorities had me down for exile here specifically. They built this body for me specially, transplanted me into it, then sent it to Earth in stasis. First thing I knew about it all was when I woke up, confused and naked, somewhere in a forest in Normandy. They'd filled my head up with human languages while I slept, so even my private thoughts were popping up in unfamiliar tongues. It was horrible." Benhard heaved himself upright and wandered through into the kitchen, to see exactly what was going on there. Matthias had covered the main work surface in salvaged plastic containers, each containing a different sample of cloudy-looking fluid. The rubbish bin was overflowing with over-the-counter pharmaceutical packaging and he was mixing liquids in a pan on the stove.

Bernhard picked up a small glass container of red liquid, which he realised was coloured vodka. The container was in the iconic shape of an Ampelmännchen; a hat-wearing man from the lights of east German pedestrian crossings. "Did you buy this?"

Matthias glanced up from his labours. "Yes. From a gift shop on Unter Den Linten. I thought it was cute; there's a little green one in there somewhere too. Maybe it fell down behind the sofa."

"Oh."

"Can you whistle?" Matthias asked.

"Whistle? Err, no, I can't. I've tried a few times."

"Me too," Matthias said, glumly returning his attention to the pan. "It's a deceptively difficult skill."

"How's this going?"

"We'll see. I've never examined human genetics before, and this lab equipment isn't exactly ideal exactly ideal for the purpose."

Bernhard nodded sadly. "Yes, you're not the first Diagrax to encounter this problem."

"It's not that I'm trying to be fussy—"

"I appreciate that."

"It's just that I couldn't salvage much from my landing site when I got here, and even the best lab equipment available on Earth wouldn't really be that much good for this purpose. Everything here's so crude."

”Not that long ago, I heard the humans have mapped their genome. Isn’t that right? Doesn’t that help at all? It’s available to everybody; they’ve put it on their internet, or something.”

“They have done that, but it’s not going to be much use here. For one thing, human ageing is called by an aggregation of factors, not a single gene. For another, to say they’ve charted *the* human genome isn’t really true, since every one of them has a unique set of coding. They’ve mapped *a* genome is all, and—“

“Okay, okay, I’ll be patient. I shouldn’t really have brought it up. For all my upbringing in a higher culture, I don’t really know any more about it than the natives here.” He paused for a breath. “You know, you should meet the other visitors here. I know you value your isolation, but, you know, I think you’d get on with them.” He fumbled with a calling card, which looked like it had been knocked up on one of those automated booths in shopping malls, and left it on the counter. It read “KREUZBERG LITERARY READING GROUP” followed by a string of telephone numbers and one or two email addresses.

“So anyway,” Matthias said, “tell me more about your arrival here?”

“I’m sure you can guess the rest. The bastards thought I was a madman and locked me up. I had no papers to prove who I was, nothing. They kept me locked in a hospital and fed me primitive drugs for the next two years. It was the most horrible experience I could imagine, looking at an alien face in the mirror, having people try to convince me I wasn’t who I believed I was… somebody called Bernhard Kuehn, who vaguely matched my vague description, was missing from West Germany, so after a while they became convinced I was that man, and why should I bother to argue with them? I stepped into Bernhard’s shoes and before I knew it, I was released from hospital and working at a bakery in Bonn.

“Of course, the authorities tried to put me in touch with my ‘family’, but the strange thing is they didn’t seem to care that much I wasn’t their lost sibling. I guess they weren’t ever that close. Can you imagine? This planet seemed like the most uncaring hellish place I could ever imagine. I drifted back into France for a bit, then came here after the Reunification.”

“Do you ever think – I mean, if you were to end up living out a human lifecycle - that your people will come back for you, rescue you from your aging human flesh and make you a Cephalus again, once they think you’ve learned your lesson?”

“I doubt it. Christ, Matthias, do you realise how far away they sent me? Our empire’s half way up the galactic arm from here. They *really* wanted me out of the way. What interest could they possibly have on a desolate rock like this?”

Matthias nodded. “So, if you don’t mind me asking, what exactly did you do wrong? Before you got exiled?”

Bernhard took a deep breath. “I was a military officer back home. Not that high-ranking, but I had subordinates. I was told I might go a long way; you know how my people are, trying to expand our influence, bringing order, reason and prosperity to the untamed systems and yadda yadda yadda.

“I was taking part in a training exercise, staged in one of our fringe systems. I was commanding a team of eight, nothing that dangerous, we just had to pass through some set waypoints and return to our base camp. There was a communications balls-up and the command officials waiting for us at my team’s waypoint instead told us to vacate the area immediately, because they were expecting a different group to touch in. We failed the mission and I was blamed for the whole thing. I tried to protest my innocence during the tribunals, but that just stirred things up all the more and they stripped me of rank and exiled me. Next thing I know, I'm in northern France, standing in a fucking shrub."

Silence descended on the kitchen, punctuated only by the simmering liquids and the bell of a tram in the street. Matthias rummaged among some containers and poured something from a jug into a drinking vessel.

"Drink this."

"What is it?"

"Coffee. There's cream and sweetener over there."

"Oh. Thanks. Well, what's your story?"

"Well, put plainly, I'm a murderer."

Bernhard choked on his drink. "You are?"

"Yep. My people no longer have laws to deal with anything like that, so I just had to make the decision to… make myself scarce."

"But how..?" Bernhard's eyes were bulging from his face. "How could something like that happen?"

"The same way it did with you. An alignment of bad circumstances and chance. Maybe a small measure of stupidity on my part, too. I tried to get as far from the Diagrax colonial region as possible, thought there would be a fairly comfortable life in one of the collectives further down the Perseus Arm, but it would have taken me forever to reach there. As it happens, my power plant gave up before I'd got even half way, and I had to home in on the nearest life-sustaining world, which happened to be this one. It's lucky that the humans broadcast their presence so recklessly by radio, I just latched onto that and it brought me right here. I managed to familiarise myself pretty well with their language and culture too, before I'd touched down.

“I ditched my ship in the Indian Ocean, just over a month ago. I swam ashore in my natural form, then just had enough plastissue from the wreck to build myself a body shell – I had to hide in trees for the first couple of days, until it was ready. I think I managed to freak out one or two of the locals, but it’s not as if anyone will believe them. I hacked some native computer networks and arranged myself a passport and some bank accounts, then headed west until I found myself here.”

Bernhard drained his mug with a slurp. ”You say you had no idea about other visitors living in Berlin, but you…” His voice was hushed and a little nervous.

“Followed my nose? Yeah, you could call it that, perhaps. I could have sniffed you out unconsciously. Or maybe it was fate.” His eyes fell involuntarily on the discarded calling card, then alighted back onto Bernhard’s face. “Maybe you were interfering with Earth’s radio media, subliminally calling me to this city. I don’t know, you tell me.”

“But you’re Diagrax… I’m sorry, but I’m still trying to understand how you can commit a human crime of murdering.”

“Believe me, so am I. Look, it’s going to take a while longer before I know if this is definitely going to work or not,” he indicated the saucepan, “maybe I should give you a call in a day or two, yeah?”

Bernhard nodded vigorously. “Okay. Okay, yes, we’ll do that.” He edged back out through the living room, towards the door.

“I’ve got your card,” Matthias called after him. There came a mumbled response, then the slam of the door.

IV

14.231.732-8

Matthias examined the paths that the cracks followed, snaking around the plaster on his bedroom ceiling. He was trying to train his body to sleep, or at least persuade the metabolism to slow down for a few hours but, good though his handiwork had been, it did not seem willing to try such things. Not capable, perhaps. Sleep was not a normal function for his species and adapting to it was no easy task. Strangely, most humans he would run into complained of sleep problems due to the current hot weather, so perhaps this was not something he should worry too much about for the moment? His discussion with Bernhard, a bit more than three Earth days earlier, also seemed to weigh on his mind. For someone who'd been initially so unwilling to discuss offworld matters in detail, he'd not had any difficulty opening up to the Cephalus. It had been too easy perhaps, and he regretted telling him so much, so soon. Outside, the sun was beneath the horizon and the city was bathed in harsh white tungsten lights and amber sodium. Sparse traffic flowed like channels of red and white liquid and a column of red lights in the sky above betrayed the looming omnipresence of TV Tower, almost eclipsing the pale disc of Earth's solitary moon. He scanned the streets for signs of human activity and wondered if he ought to go for a walk to clear his head.

The small apartment was already becoming cluttered with junk. From retro knick-knack shops around Oderberger Straße, he had been scavenging strange bits of half-obsolete technology that might have made the East Germans envious during the country's division, but now just looked a bit sad. His portable television for instance, with its peeling wood-effect covering, had a slot for playing audio cassettes, yet there was no obvious reason why a television might need this attribute. Next to it sat a grimy lava lamp full of faded liquid, which forever struggled to move inside the glass. Around the floor now sat neat stacks of dog-eared science paperbacks and a stereo turntable with built in eight-track tape deck and AM radio had now been converted, with the aid of some coat hangers, into a crude centrifuge for experimenting with jars of fluid. By day, the set-up looked a little comical, but by the light from outside the window, the massed books and other structures took on a ghostly new appearance, looking almost like a miniature fractal copy of the Berlin cityscape as he looked down on it from above. It was oddly reassuring how the universe arranged its scales in this curious Russian-doll style.

There was a buzz of activity within the miniature city on his carpet. A rhythmic buzzing, accompanied by a bright green light. He tracked its source through the untidy streets and located his phone, which he'd left on silent mode a few days earlier. The screen reported an incoming call from a number he didn't recognise.

"Hallo? Who's this?"

A woman's voice came from the tiny speaker, clipped but with a sound that was not unfriendly. "Good evening, am I speaking to Matthias?"

"You are. And who am I speaking with?"

"You don't know me, but my name is Sonja. I'm sorry to call you at such an hour."

"It's fine."

"I'm a friend of Bernhard."

"Ahh, Bernhard," he noted an unintentional change in the tone of his own voice. "How is he? Well, I hope?"

“He’s well. I’ve heard you’ve been assisting him in the last few days?”

That was an awkward question, coming from a stranger. Matthias cursed silently, wishing he’d established this woman’s relationship to Bernhard, before she’d asked something like this. It would be too risky to simply bluff his way through; there was nothing for it but to ask outright. “Are you related to Bernhard? Or do you care for him in some way?”

“Care or him? Well, I suppose I should introduce myself properly…” it was her turn now to sound a little pained. “You understand my meaning if I say *Cephalus*?”

“Umm… It’s a word he’s used around me.”

“Matthias, I am a Diagrax. I’ve been living on this planet for seventy-two years.”

He took a deep breath. There could be little doubt she was calling him from the ‘literary group’, but this didn’t make him feel a lot more relaxed about telling her things. One possibility, which germinated right then at the back of his mind, was that she was a curious human, who head perhaps stumbled onto the group by chance and was now researching a story about some group-delusional nutters, to sell to a newspaper? There were tabloids in this city, or national ones for that matter, who would stoop to such things. Maybe Thomas had decided his tales of an alien culture were more than just hypothetical and had put her onto him.

“I’m helping Bernhard with a project, but he’s asked me to keep it a private matter.”

“He wants you to extend his lifespan, doesn’t he? It’s alright, he’s asked me about it too. I tried and failed some time ago.”

“Right.” He sat down heavily on the bed. Not much point in being cagey then, if she already knows this much. “Well, how nice to speak to a Diagrax after all this time.”

“There are a few of us—Bernhard told you about the reading group, right? – There’s a group of us out in town for drinks right now, we thought it might be nice if you come and join us?”

Bernhard had mentioned a group comprising several species; how typical that they should nominate a member of his own to call him and invite him out. Still, he thought, if Bernhard had passed on the story about him purposely killing another sentient being, then it seemed strange that any of them would even want to meet him. He’d half hoped for this when he first mentioned the fact.

Well, there was nothing for it now; they clearly weren’t going to leave him alone until he showed his face to them. Even on a planet this remote and wretched, there was nowhere to hide.

“Okay, where shall I find you?”

* * * *

It was a weeknight and the U-Bahn had just stopped running by this time, but Matthias found his way to them easily enough, by one of the twenty-four hour tram routes. A group of six were sitting around a table in a small, dimly lit bar in a back road close to Alexanderplatz. The place was curiously decorated, with its walls tiled in a way that suggested it might have once been a butcher’s shop, long ago. Its more recent owners had filled it with mismatched old furniture and set up some subdued lighting, candles and a spinning disco ball, with speakers in each corner that blared out rock music.

A bust of Lenin gazed balefully down from a shelf above the bar and a big, shaggy black dog glanced upwards from the floor where it rested.

"Matthias!" The woman who waved to him first was sprightly and in her late twenties, a bright white smile and piercing green eyes that parted a cascade of dark brown curls. As she got up to attract his attention, all conversation at the table ceased and the other five appraised him silently. Having spent all his time on Earth so far trying to be inconspicuous, he approached them gingerly, at a loss for what to say.

"Come on, come on! Join us!

"Thank you."

"I'm Sonja, have a seat, I'll introduce you to the group."

Matthias did as he was instructed.

"As you know, I'm a Diagrax, like yourself. This is Dylan," she paused to indicate a heavily built and unusually tall man in his late thirties, with olive skin and dark eyes. "He is a Hydgol. He has been on Earth the longest out of all of us."

The man nodded curtly and spoke with a rumbling voice. "And doesn't it feel like it!"

There was a rumble of laughter from around the table, although Matthias couldn't help wondering how many times Dylan might have made that joke in the past.

Sonja's hand moved on to a pair of women who appeared to be from southern Asia, slightly weathered faces framed by dark locks and elaborate silver jewellery. They did not look alike enough to be sisters, but they both moved at the same time to offer wary smiles. "This is Ingrid and Leandra, of the Robokind. They are researchers who have travelled here all the way from the Crux Scutum Arm."

"Pleased to meet you."

A younger man was indicted next; a bespectacled, energetic-looking and prematurely balding beanpole of an individual. "Torsten," he said, thrusting out his hand, before Sonja had a chance to introduce him.

Matthias shook the man's hand, restating his own name again, in a way which he hoped was most appropriate.

"Torsten is of a race called the Nitid," Sonja explained.

"A Nitid? I'm afraid you have me at a disadvantage," Matthias grinned awkwardly. "I've not heard your people mentioned before."

"Unsurprising, we come from an obscure star system."

"Well, nice to meet you Torsten."

"And last but not least, we have Simone, who is of the Wormkind." The last of the group was a thin, elderly black woman, whose grey hair was dragged back into a tight bun, possibly in an attempt to smooth out her facial features. She rose to her feet with some difficulty and leant forward over the table, cupping both hands around Matthias's with a surprisingly firm grip.

"A pleasure that you could come here."

Sonja turned to face him. "You can metabolise human food and drink?"

"Sure."

She pushed a glass of red wine towards him. "Good, we've been keeping that safe for you. Of course, this is not the whole group, but some of us have been unwell, or have other commitments tonight. You know, there's been a lot of talk about you for the last few days. Your arrival's made you quite a celebrity here."

"I was the last to arrive before you," Torsten added, "I've been here for two years now. How did you find your way here? Did you get lost?"

"No. No, I was trying to reach somewhere else and I had a problem with my ship. I was exiled by my—" he corrected himself, glancing at Sonja. "*our* people. Look, I'm not sure how much Bernhard told you—"

At the mention of Bernhard, the atmosphere around the table changed noticeably. The CD being played by the barman had finished, and a candle near the table chose an inappropriate moment to hiss noisily.

"Poor Bernhard," said Simone. "It's good of you to try and help him."

"Well, I'm doing what I can, you know."

"The Cephalus regime is not known for their light handedness with those who displease them," added Leandra, sadly. "In fact, they remind me so much of some human governments."

There were a few grunts of approval.

"They don't change," agreed Dylan. "I should know, I survived both world wars and the ones against Napoleon the century before that. Believe me, for every human trying to change their world for the better, there's at least another prepared to corrupt it all back to the stone age for their own short-term profit."

Matthias still caught the pervading sense that these conversations had been repeated many times and were possibly just being spooled out again now for his benefit. He thought he saw eyes turned surreptitiously in his direction, to gauge his reaction to these well-established topics.

“Where do you think Saddam Hussein’s hiding?” Asked Torsten. “Do you think the Americans will ever catch him?”

Matthias shrugged. “I don’t know. Hiding in a hole somewhere probably, with his little shopping bag full of Weapons of Mass Destruction. His two sons died yesterday, did you see that in the news?”

“They won’t find him,” Ingrid said with a snort, “he probably slipped the net some time ago. By now I expect he’s in Pakistan or somewhere, smoking cigars with Bin Laden. Well, either that or already dead. Perhaps he’ll be like Hitler, his body never officially found. Won’t that be fun, we’ll spend the next thirty years reading in the tabloids that he’s been sighted on the moon.”

Simone nodded. ”In today’s newspaper, it says a third of Germans under thirty believe the American government crashed those planes into their World Trade Centre. Can you believe that?”

“Americans are such an easy target these days,” laughed Dylan, “if the other nations aren’t blaming them for the world’s conspired wrongs, they’re blaming aliens!”

This got another round of laughter and Matthias joined in too, although he wondered if perhaps he’d heard English being spoken at the table behind where he sat. Probably a group of tourists. They didn’t seem to be paying much attention to the rest of the bar, anyway.

“So, is Berlin the capital for offworld visitors to live?” Matthias felt awkward asking this, but it needed to be asked.

“I suppose you could say it is,” smiled Sonja. “Of course, not everyone comes here. No-one knows exactly how many visitors there are on this planet right now – we don’t all talk to each other - but we agree it can’t be more than fifty, at the very most.”

“It’s moved around over the years,” Dylan added. “Our group’s changed location a few times, as circumstances dictate. You know, we all had a bit of a fright in ninety-five, or whenever it was, when that film footage surfaced of an alien autopsy. It didn’t look like any race we’d seen before, but it fooled us for a while, just like it did most of the humans; we thought the anonymity of offworlders was about to be fucked.” He laughed, but the sound lacked humour.

Simone leant forward, her cracked old voice hushed. “It’s not that we’ve ever had problems with being found out, but we find it *unhealthy* to group together for too long in any one place. For a few years here and there it’s fine, but it’s not wise to put down too many roots in one place. Eventually people might sniff us out.”

V

14.231.733-0

A couple of hours had passed at the bar, then the group decided to split and go different ways. Sonja wanted to check out a nightclub nearby, although this idea did not sit well with other members of the group, particularly with Simone who, despite her youthful vigour, looked far too old to be in such a place. She was, like Matthias, un-aging, although her human bodyshell would run through a 'normal' lifecycle and then need to be renewed by an internal process, hence its current state of decrepitude.

It was eventually only Matthias and Torsten who agreed to visit this place with her, although she didn't seem too disappointed. The other four left the bar with them, then turned off down a different street, heading for Simone's apartment, where they would while away the rest of the night in their usual fashion, by talking and playing music.

"We'll see if we can find you later," Sonja called over her shoulder as they disappeared, then led the two men through a labyrinth of deserted streets and past the colossal concrete base of the TV Tower, to a row of railway arches, from which a steady bass throb was emanating. A group of club-goers skulked and sat on the pavement by one arch, outside an unassuming metal door, through which pulsing lights could be seen. The revellers, clearly lacking a proper designated chill-out area, were smoking cigarettes, drinking beers and spirits from plastic cups or just taking a break from the packed interior of the place. They all wore combinations of, mostly black, fishnet, PVC or fabric which was laden with unnecessary fasteners. The smell of sweat secretions drifted in and out of the press of bodies, mingling with the dry ice and cigarette smoke.

“Are they going to let us in here?” Torsten whispered. “I feel a bit underdressed. I’m not really used to this sort of place.”

Sonja led the way through the crowd to the door regardless and the security guard gave them a questioning look, but charged them each three Euros and let them through. The cramped interior was indeed full to bursting with people and to a newcomer whose research into Earth’s more obscure Western musical subcultures was woefully incomplete, the place seemed more than a bit perplexing. Above the metal encrusted human faces and strangely styled hair, loomed a number of bizarre sculptures, sitting atop pedestals and hanging from the underside of the arch on wires. They depicted warped human forms, fused with gas masks, computer keyboards and other mechanical junk, all of which were sprayed silver.

“Interesting place,” he commented to Sonja, his voice raised above the industrial music.

“It’s not disappointing me so far.” She looked around for the signs pointing to the restrooms. “Look, I’m going to try and find somewhere to score. Do you think you could check the men’s toilets? I don’t think a place like this has attendants.”

“I’m sorry?”

“Recreational drugs. They affect your body shell, don’t they?”

“I’d assume so. I’ve not tried before. Probably some of the active chemicals would be processed and absorbed into my own bloodstream—“

“Great stuff. Looks like Torsten’s gone for a dance, I’m sure he’ll be okay on his own for a bit. Meet you back over here in a few minutes, yeah?” She brushed her hand against his thigh, turned and disappeared into the crowd. Matthias lingered where he was for a few moments, confused, then went looking for the men’s room.

For all the density of the crowd inside the club, he found the men's room to be relatively empty. Perhaps some of the clientele found it more convenient to urinate in the street? During his time in human form, Matthias had not become fully accustomed yet to certain bodily functions, finding them a little confusing and distasteful. One man was standing in front of the mirror making a fairly futile-looking attempt to control his floppy curtains of dyed-black hair and Matthias approached him in a way which he hoped wouldn't seem shifty. The music was muffled in here and a conversation was less problematic, but he worried about being overheard. This seemed like an invitation to be either arrested or ripped off.

"Do you know how I can score near here?"

The man regarded him with pale, confused-looking eyes and mumbled that he didn't speak much German.

"No problem," Matthias responded, switching to English. "Is this okay?"

"Yeah, uhh, sorry, what were you asking?"

"I was asking about drugs; I don't suppose you…"

The man shook his head sadly. "I wish I did; don't really know much I'm afraid, I'm *Auslander*."

"Okay, it's fine. I'm Swiss, so I know what you mean. You American?"

"No, English. Don't really know who best to ask about drugs around here, I'm still finding my way."

Matthias smiled thinly, turned and left. That guy had seemed so lost and uneasy there, wandering around on his own, like he was a million miles from his homeland.

“Are you okay for drinks?” Matthias asked Torsten a while later, shouting over the din of the music once more. Sonja hadn’t yet reappeared, although his own search for a dealer by the toilet stalls had been short and fruitless. Not that he’d really been sure what he was looking for, anyway. Perhaps Sonja had been luckier? Biding his time, he’d decided to get a round of drinks in.

“Sure,” Torsten bounced, his thinning hair glistening with beads of sweat. “Bring it on. Vodka, please. And lots of ice.”

Matthias had almost made it to the front of the press of bodies around the bar, when he felt a tap on his shoulder. It was Sonja, but she looked concerned.

“I found some pills,” she whispered. Her mouth was against his ear to make the words audible, although he suspected she also wanted him to feel her breath. “We should leave soon, though. The woman who sold me these thinks there’s going to be a police raid, maybe in an hour or two.”

“I see. Okay, then. This place is fun, but it’s a bit of a culture shock. More so than elsewhere.” His eyes scanned the edge of the nearest dance floor and caught sight of Torsten dancing by himself, moving his long skinny limbs in time to the music, almost as if he were having a spasm, as he waited for his next drink. “I think maybe he’s had enough for one night, anyway.”

“Okay, we make a move in a few minutes, then.” Her smile returned. “I need to get outside and cool down. It’s great that I’ve had a chance to meet you, it’s been so long since I was near another like me.”

”Look, now that we’re away from the others, how much exactly did Bernhard tell you about me? And my past?”

"Not a lot. I want to know all the details though. We've got all the time in the world!"

"When I first met Bernhard, he implied there were others of our kind here. Is that true?"

"As far as I know. Well, there was one other; I haven't seen her for a few years now. She went a bit… well, funny in the head and went off to be alone. Nobody's heard from her since she left the group. I suppose some of us adjust to life here better than others."

"I can imagine that. I… don't really know a lot about your group, and it's not that I think I'd dislike any of you, but do you spend a lot of time together at the expense of socialising with the humans?"

Sonja's face contorted as she thought about the question. "Perhaps. But trust me, after spending a lot of time alone amongst these creatures, you'll really start to feel claustrophobic and miss having offworlders with you. I was here for *sixteen years* before they discovered me by chance. You're lucky."

VI

14.231.733-2

The journey from the city centre to Simone's apartment was not a long one, but they were impeded on the way by trying to support Torsten, who, was now burbling incoherently and had to stop twice to be sick. It didn't bother Matthias or Sonja too much, as they were by now basking in a warm, happy glow from the drugs and they spoke excitedly about the more obscure aspects of human music, art and literature. As the sky began to lighten very slightly and deserted offices and shopping areas gave way to graffiti-spattered residential streets, Sonja stopped by a door to a tenement and jabbed at the buzzer. A deeper buzz responded a few seconds later and they pushed open the door, each holding one of Torsten's arms to stop him crashing through parked bicycles and sprawling on the cement floor of the hallway.

They made even more laboured progress up echoing stairs to the second floor landing, where Ingrid and Leandra met them in a light-spilling open doorway, forefingers clamped to lips as they ushered the trio inside.

"Have a seat," Simone smiled. The living room was large, with a high ceiling typical of Berlin's late nineteenth century architecture, fortunate enough to have survived the wars. Strangely, it was painted entirely white and the furniture matched this too. Four well-worn white leather sofas backed against every wall and there seemed to be a party in progress, with all the members of the Kreuzberg Literary Reading Group attending, including some who'd not made it to the bar earlier.

"Has Torsten had a good night?" She enquired.

“Yuhh-huh.” He answered, curling up in a ball on a pile of cushions, while Leandra fetched him a coffee and a glass of iced water.

Matthias dutifully took one of the vacant spaces, feeling a pang of disappointment that there was no space available next to Sonja. As he was unfamiliar with human courtship practice – or at least he was unsure how to separate the fact from the copious amounts of fiction he’d unearthed – he didn’t know what level of body contact was appropriate, although he’d stroked her back a few times as they walked from the club, which she hadn’t seemed to mind. He wondered if he would feel attracted to her in her natural form; was her human form a close analogue to the Diagrax body she’d been born with? He had asked – awkwardly – if she was female inside that body shell and she’d laughed and assured him that she was. From across the room now, he saw her distributing the remaining ecstasy pills among the others.

Bernhard was among those present, although he didn’t seem terribly aware of the others around him. He sat on the floor, his back resting on the seat of one sofa, gazing at the ceiling while he slowly swilled some wine around, rhythmically, in a glass. Matthias noticed, for the first time, that some opera music was playing quietly from a small stereo in the corner of the room, and this seemed to be holding Bernhard in a semi-drunken trance. Either that, he supposed, or the Cephalus just wasn’t feeling communicative. Maybe he suspected the anti-ageing research wasn’t going well, and was pissed off about it? Close to him, Torsten was already nearly asleep.

A small dressing table stood in one corner, wedged in by two of the sofas. On it stood several glass flutes, most of them empty, but four contained about a centimetre and half of viscous, amber fluid which obviously wasn’t champagne. Three of these were now distributed among the new-comers, Torsten presumably being too out of it to appreciate his. Matthias clasped the narrow stem in his hand and tilted the glass this way and that, watching the strange effect with which the light sources reflected on and seemingly swam lazily through the oily stuff inside. It had no detectible odour.

"Drink," Sonja whispered. It had a faintly chemical taste, although Matthias cursed the fact that his human palette registered flavours differently. He didn't *think* he'd ever tried this off-world, but it was hard to think where else the strange drink might have come from. It disappeared down his throat with a warm, tingly sensation.

Matthias returned his attention to Simone who, he realised, had been running through a list of names of all the other offworlders he'd not yet been introduced to. Although he missed the first few introductions – if Simone noticed he'd been inattentive, she didn't seem bothered by it – he got the impression that the Robokind made up around half the total group and, perhaps, the majority of all offworlders currently living on the Earth. Everybody presented welcoming smiles. He wondered if the lingering effect of the drug was still causing him to smile back at them like an idiot. The muscles in his cheeks were beginning to feel tired, but there was no mirror nearby to check.

"This looks like the direction in which music technology's going, at least for the foreseeable future," Dylan was saying to a short, wiry black Robokind man, who was fidgeting with a small white plastic box.

"It's been interesting to watch; you know, I've seen the whole evolution of sound recording on this planet, from wax cylinders up to these pods, and the diversity of techniques for distributing music has led to such a growth in genres and styles. I wish someone could have objectively studied musical development like that on my own world."

"They're called *iPods*."

"Whatever. I think they're now reaching a plateau where media can be disseminated so freely between human cultures… iPods. Sounds like something from one of those *Men In Black* movies."

This brought a chorus of chuckling.

"Next time I reincarnate here, I want to choose a pug bodyshell, just like the guy in that film!" Simone added. "I've often wondered what it's like to be a dog. Some of them seem to have cushier lives around here than the humans do."

"How's the research going, Matthias?" It took a moment for Matthias to detune himself from the music discussion and refocus his attention on Bernhard, who was now addressing him. "It's been getting a bit intensive. I needed to take a break for a little while. You know, I think coming out tonight and meeting all these people has actually done me some good."

"Ah."

"But the work itself… I don't know. There are still some avenues I need to pursue, but I have to be honest, nothing's shown any positive results this far. I may have better know-how than the humans, but they do have access to better equipment…" His voice trailed off as he tried to think of a more hopeful direction in which to steer the discussion. Bernhard continued to study his face, expectantly.

"My field back home was more in agricultural engineering," Sonja broke in. "Human genetics is very interesting, but without any grounding in alien physiology, I didn't know where to start. They're similar to us, in how they're constructed, same sort of base pair combinations, yet they're also so very different."

Bernhard took another sip of his wine. "Well they can't even figure themselves out, and I've been watching them try for most of the time I've been stuck here. I've been reading their science journals, sometimes there's a mention of a new theory or a supposed breakthrough, but I think if they ever do manage to conquer, or even substantially delay their own mortality, it's going to be far too late for me."

"You don't know that."

"I strongly doubt they'll get it right. Look at them, they're always a step away from annihilating themselves anyway. It'd probably do us all a favour if they did, frankly, what's a species like this got to contribute if they do make it to a post-utopian level and begin colonising other systems?"

Not really wishing to get drawn into such topics, Matthias shrugged politely.

"I feel sorry for the species that share this planet with them right now – those that they haven't already made extinct – so I hardly think anyone will benefit from an interstellar human presence."

"Maybe not yet," interjected the Robokind sitting next to Dylan, "but their culture's still developing. As a knock-on effect of controlling their mortality, it's not that impossible that one day they'll produce real intelligence-boosting drugs, or achieve this through direct manipulation of their genes... or, of course, transference of their minds to other, bigger vessels, as my own race did. What we're seeing around us now might just be the larval stage, an early prototype, of what the mature species will be like."

"Might," Bernhard reminded him. "My people sent me here as punishment, so that must say something about humanity's prospects."

"Now that sort of thinking isn't going to help anyone," Simone broke in. "Come on, you know the score, most of us are here on this world without any immediate way off, it may not be perfect but all we can do is come to make peace with—"

“Skirr is in agreement with me.”

“Who’s Skirr?” Matthias asked.

“Another Cephalus. I’m not alone here, you know—well, I *almost* am.” This seemed to draw further dismayed looks from the others, but he paid no attention to them. “He’s… not quite right. But that’s what being on this rock for a few decades too many does to a sentient being. Skirr doesn’t get out much nowadays.

“Diagrax gut bacteria. Now, that must be toxic to humans.” Bernhard breathed, a strange gleam in his eyes. “You two must have the means to wipe them all out. Right there, inside you. If we extracted some cultures from you and released it… my god, can you imagine it? Their medicine would be totally ill-prepared for that. We’d wipe the surface clean within a couple of years I reckon, have a nice virgin planet again—“

Simone’s aged face now crumpled into an angry grimace. “Stop it.”

“It’d serve them all right. We’d have all this as our playground; perhaps, with a bit of tinkering, we could make the bug toxic to humans only, leave all the non-sentient species. We could be rulers. Wouldn’t need to pull a trigger. And think of the favour we’d have done to other emerging cultures, who won’t ever have to meet them”

Sonja stood up. ”I’m leaving.”

The warm buzz of the chemicals in Matthias’s blood stream seemed to have been dispelled by the sour atmosphere he now found himself in. He watched Sonja for a few moments, gauging whether or not this was likely to be a bluff.

Bernhard raised his hands in submission. “Hey, I’m not saying we should do any of this. You know I wouldn’t, however bad things get. But you have to admit, the thought’s crossed your minds at some point. For everything they've achieved here, they're incredibly vulnerable and naive. They're more than capable of doing it to themselves one way or another anyway, dumb bastards don't need our help."

He heaved himself up and went into the kitchen to look for more drink. Sonja and Matthias exchanged awkward glances. "He's just bitter," she whispered.

"Please stay," pleased Ingrid, "we'd love to know more about our new Diagrax. In fact," she flashed a glance towards Simone, "I think we were planning to open up in a short while, since we haven't done for such a long time, and it would be a proper initiation for the newer members."

Sonja lingered uncertainly.

"What do you mean by 'open up'?" Matthias asked.

A hint of warmth returned to Sonja's face. "Yes, that would be lovely. Then we can see each other properly. I don't think *all* of us have participated yet. Well, some of us can't, if we're totally sealed in, but the rest of us."

Simone had taken up a position, leaning with her upper back against the wall in one corner, and she had hold of the hem of her dress, which she was unselfconsciously pulling upwards.

"What's she doing?" Matthias whispered, but Sonja shushed him. The old woman cast away her outer clothing and rested, perfectly motionless, against the wall, with tracts of sagging old brown skin disclosed between her undergarments. Her face appeared blank, eyes rolled back. He nervously glanced over to some of the other book club members, hoping to gauge their reactions. Some seemed only mildly interested, others – the Robokind in particular – had taken on similar trance-like appearances.

There was a silence which seemed to last an eternity. Then a faint sound like claws dragging on cloth emanated first from Leandra then, one by one, from other Robokind. Leandra hastily unbuttoned her silk blouse and unhooked her bra, but Matthias's eyes were already being drawn to a flat, circular area of elevated skin in her abdomen, which was growing more pronounced by the second. Her fellows did the same and, after almost a minute, there were a series of escaping gas hisses and circular hatches swung open – Matthias couldn't help being reminded of front-loading washing machines – and dark, crawling things began to awkwardly emerge, hauling themselves into the open from dark interiors. The host bodies now lay motionless while several clanking, whirring, spider-like contraptions scurried around on the sofas and dropped to the carpet. How many were there? There seemed to be at least three or four inside each host. They moved with unsettling purpose to the centre of the room and met in a haphazard bundle of waving claws and pencil-thin legs. For a short while, this seemed to be all the creatures had longed for, to touch each other physically once more, but then a new order became apparent in their actions, as the mechanical limbs meshed together and formed complex, rigid structures. A single tall, gangly tower began to arise from a circular base and when the last of the tiny multi-legged robots settled into place at the top, a composite body had taken shape; a four-foot high tapering stalk with a cluster of lenses and tendrils emerging from a bulb at the top, which appeared to be the creature's head. Its numerous eyes swept the room, taking in its audience and the limp, semi-naked, husks of its host bodies, circular openings still gaping and scattered around amongst items of equally discarded clothing.

The awed silence was broken first by Dylan's huge hands clapping, then by everybody else in the room who was still able to do so. Bernhard leant against the kitchen doorframe, wearing a fairly forced-looking smile of appreciation. Matthias wondered how self-conscious they might all feel doing this, and whether alcohol or drug-taking earlier in the night might have lowered their inhibitions.

"Does that feel good?" Sonja beamed.

The dark stalk made a cacophony of small chittering sounds, then it took a bow and said *yes*. The word seemed to have been vibrated by a hundred tiny cricket legs rather than produced vocally, which struck Matthias as profoundly unsettling, but it was at least intelligible.

In the corner of the room, Simone's body gave a tremor but she remained in her trance, facial muscles occasionally bunching with effort as she tried to maintain control over some incredibly complex process. For no reason that he was able to place, Matthias thought of the big, famous signpost that had been preserved at Checkpoint Charlie, but now it vividly proclaimed in his mind's eye – in English, German, French and Russian – "YOU ARE NOW LEAVING THE HUMAN SECTOR." He stifled a stupid grunt of a laugh and hoped nobody else had noticed.

Sonja now got down on her knees and unbuttoned her blouse, flinging it into one of the piles of abandoned clothing. Presumably, despite the time she'd spent living inside it, she still did not regard the human body as her own and felt little shame in having it in full view. She lent forward, curling herself into a tight ball, with her head against the floor and the bumps of her vertebrae showing through the smooth, taut skin of her taut back. He saw various muscles tense, then her body gave a sound which was reminiscent of the scraping he'd heard the Robokind produce a few minutes earlier. This was more familiar though, and he suspected what would happen next. The noise gave way to a louder, intermittent splitting and popping, then the skin began to part along the axis of her spine. The muscle and other tissues beneath divided with some reluctance, with some glistening filaments still trying to connect them, until the real Sonja began to uncoil and emerge from inside. Matthias's heart leapt to see this once familiar body shape again; primitive Earth cultures might have called her a serpent, but her clusters of long, multi-jointed limbs soon unfurled from her upper body and broke up the flowing-snakelike outline. Her jaws opened, loudly sucking in a breath of the Earth's air and displaying banks of needle-thin teeth, while four eyes, dark as blobs of crude oil, independently pivoted from face to face in the audience. He felt happier than he'd done for centuries; she was indeed beautiful.

There was a crack from the corner and eyes turned to watch Simone, who now had a star-shaped split opening in her belly. Somewhere within, a membrane burst and some watery liquid gushed out through the new opening. As the triangular flaps of skin peeled back, a dozen black, shiny, eel-like creatures emerged and flopped onto the damp carpet. Somebody in the room let out a blood curdling shriek; it was a sound from a human throat and Matthias looked around in confusion for the source, before he realised it was Torsten, who had woken from his stupor and now pointed a hysterical, accusing finger at the scene before him, while clumsily climbing the back of the sofa with his other three limbs to get as far from the alien beings as possible. His eyes were open so wide, they looked as if they would drop from their orbits and roll away.

"This isn't right." Presumably Torsten was addressing everyone present, but he didn't take his eyes from the cluster of eels, the mechanical stalk and the serpent in the middle of the room. His feet stood on the sofa cushions, as if this might afford him some protection from the smaller creatures, in case they tried to jump up and reach him. Sonja regarded him with a Diagrax expression which Matthias knew signified pity, but she would not be able to make human vocal speech outside of her body shell.

It was Dylan who spoke to him first, his attention refocused from his own transformation onto the room around him. "Torsten?" he asked, his rumbling voice made softer than usual. "What's the matter?"

"You're all sick!" Torsten's voice sounded hoarse, as if he'd been punched in the stomach. He repeated himself, a little louder this time, but still not with the shout he was clearly trying to muster.

"Sit down." Matthias heard himself say.

Torsten shook his head. "There's no way I'm staying with these things around. My god… my god, you've been like this all this time. All this time! And I just played along because I thought—" the words he was looking for caught in his throat. He crabbed sideways along the sofa, getting ready to jump down and run in the direction of the door. *"My god, it's all for real!"*

Matthias had started to feel a little light-headed, but he run across the room to bar his exit, stumbling over an abandoned shoe an almost falling. He reached the threshold to the room just in time, legs splayed and palms resting on opposite sides of the doorframe. Despite not being heavily built, he expected to be more than a match for a scrawny individual like Torsten. The only other way he could now escape would be through one of the windows which, unfortunately, did not seem impossible given his crazed state of mind. If he tried that, it was questionable if he'd survive.

A deathly silence descended on the room, interrupted only by the CD player and a moist squirming sound as the dark eels that formed Simone's collective 'self' slithered back up her human legs towards the safety of her body cavity. They had obviously not foreseen this and had left themselves dangerously exposed, a problem exacerbated by their slow crawling speed. All eyes were on the human intruder, wondering what his next move would be. Realising he was trapped, he slowly sank to his knees and curled into a fetal position, muttering “don’t hurt me.” There was a whooshing sound like a fire extinguisher and a narrow jet of white vapour shot from the head of the Robokind stalk, engulfing Torsten for a few seconds in a small cloud, which dissipated into drifting snowflakes and then vanished completely. The man twitched a few times and made gasping sounds, then lay perfectly still on the floor.

Matthias stumbled and sat down. The room had started to spin and he was having difficulty judging distances between things, although the dizzy sensation was oddly quite enjoyable.

He’ll be unconscious for a few hours, the stalk announced while all eyes were on the unmoving body, a short eternity away across the chasm of the living room.

“Looks like there’s no such thing as a Nitid after all,” Dylan said, sadly.

VII

14.231.734-1

Matthias awoke to the rumble of traffic outside and some synthesizer music playing quietly from an old clock radio close to his bed. The alarm had not gone off; he would not expect it to, since the mechanism which flipped over the faces of the 'digital' display had long since jammed. He sat up, feeling a little sluggish, then realised how odd it was that he'd been unconscious at all. Had something happened to his human body shell, to make it zone out like that?

Sonja emerged from the kitchen, stepping carefully around the piles of books and old electronics, wrapped in a trailing bath towel. She held a steaming mug.

"How are you feeling?" She asked.

"Umm, alright, I think. How long was I sleeping for?" He consulted his memory bionics about the tune he could hear and they reported back that it was the *Beverly Hills Cop* theme tune. Why any radio station would play that, they couldn't so easily advise.

"About six hours. Not far off average, for an adult human."

That last comment sent a wave of panic through him, as he remembered the events of the previous night. He protested, "But I'm—"

He stopped, as the memory re-crystallised in his mind. After Torsten's limp body had been moved to another room and the sun had continued to rise and fill the room with its yellow-tinged light, the festivities had resumed and he too had 'opened up', joining the others in the melee of contrasting physical forms in the white room. For the first time in an eternity, he looked through his own eyes, instead of perceiving the colour spectrum of a human retina. He had witnessed sights which, even before he had visited the Earth, he would have found surprising. A Hydgol! A creature of which he knew so little, rising from Dylan's chest, like an squirming pink mandrake root, so small and vulnerable-looking next to the bodyshell which housed it; its delicate head remained encased in a mirrored breathing helmet. Wriggling black snake-like forms that made up the physical nodes of Simone's composite mind. Mechanical life in its ever-changing amorphous complexity… and he and Sonja getting to know each other rather better. He'd found the coupling a great deal less fussy and laboured in their natural bodies.

Sonja pointed to the clock radio, which he now noticed had been repaired. "The human philosopher, Jean-Paul Satre, once said 'Three o'clock is always too late or too early for anything you want to do.'"

"I think he was right," Matthias said, "not that I've really got my head around the local units of measurement, so far." He paused, looking up at the window for a few moments to watch a distant plane crossing the azure sky. "Thanks for last night. It was certainly an eye-opener. In a good way. What was that yellow stuff we drank?"

"You liked it? That's a very precious commodity, all the more so on this planet."

"I think, after it started to kick in, it was like…" his voice trailed away as he fished for the right words to describe the experience. "I don't know. I think, after everything else, my senses must have been a bit screwed up anyway, but I really can't say I've felt anything quite like that anywhere. It was like my veins were pumping warm honey instead of blood."

She laughed. "That's a good description. I could never have too much of that feeling; if only the damn stuff wasn't so hard to find." She smiled, but her expression seemed oddly distant for a moment. "Right, I'm making blackcurrant tea. Or, at least, I'm trying to. Want some? It's a bit difficult to find anything here."

"Sorry about that."

"You seemed to be having a good time last night. I couldn't let you visit this city without experiencing the Book Club. But… you almost did, didn't you?"

"Yeah. I'd been trying to avoid other non-humans. If truth be told, I didn't want that much contact with humans either, but most of the learning I'd hoped to do here required me to be in an urban environment."

"I… thought you were trying to avoid contact with us, yes. Is there some reason you wanted to tell me? Perhaps now's a better time to discuss that."

He'd expected this topic to arise soon, and was grateful for the extra time he'd had to run through the explanation in his head. If he'd gone ahead with telling her in the noisy club earlier, it might have sounded a little too blunt. "Sonja, which planet were you born on?"

She hesitated, trying to remember the clumsy human astronomical name for her home (human and Diagrax pronunciations being mutually impossible with the others' vocal apparatus). "Psi^5 Aurigae 12B."

That made sense. He thought she had the mannerisms of a solid-worlder. A few hours earlier, when he'd watched her shed her human skin, he'd noticed how her body bore adaptations for a higher gravity environment. "You grew up there? If so, you're lucky. I lived most of my life in the Lambda system, on one of the twenty-seven artificial worlds there. Have you ever seen one?"

She shook her head. "No, only heard about them. They sounded nice."

"Not that nice. Billions of us, sandwiched together inside a load of concentric spheres of rock, the largest of which was about ten thousand kilometres in diameter. We had oceans to swim in, but can you imagine living in a sea where the only sky you can ever look at above is a load of stonework and metal, covered in buttresses and artificial lights?"

She looked shocked. "Why pack so many together?"

"Our crap excuse for a central government – I dislike them, in case I've not mentioned that already – thinks it's a good idea to overpopulate our fringe systems, to discourage other empires from wanting to build planetoids there. A few thousand years ago, they sent a fleet to my neighbourhood to set up big-scale mines and hydroponic farms and kickstart massive population breeding programmes, essentially just so they could have a bulwark against races like the Cephalus expanding further down our spiral arm."

Matthias still had much practice to do with reading human facial expressions, but he wondered from Sonja's right now if she'd ever had reason to question the Diagrax hierarchy before. Possibly, she'd not. "Look, how about you tell me how you came to be on this world?"

Sonja tried to shrug off the perplexed look and then launched into her own tale. "Well, there's not that much to tell, I suppose. I was involved in various social research programmes for a few years and more and more of my work touched on how the primitive development stages a culture can influence its strengths and weaknesses after it reaches maturity. I gained approval to do some field research, which wasn't that difficult to get, considering I wanted to work alone and without any specialised equipment. I headed out towards the rim, looking for developing systems which, ideally were just beginning their first industrial phase. I didn't find any specifically at that point - it was 1933 when I reached Earth – but this seemed to be the closest example I was likely to find, and luckily the humans keep enough records for me to fill in the gaps of what history I missed." She shrugged – the story was at an end. "And here I am. I lived in America during the big war, keeping out of the way and observing from a distance. It was harder to scratch a living back then, as all official documents were on paper and it wasn't so easy to falsify data, especially with all the paranoia that was drifting about. I picked up most of what I knew about their culture by sitting in libraries and cinemas, and censorship was so stiff back then, it really did take me a long while to pick certain things up. But I made do and, you know, I think there's quite a comfortable difficulty curve with living on this rock. It was a really happy day for me though, when the other offworlders made contact with me and we founded the Book Club. Sometimes I wonder, if it wasn't for that, whether the humans would have driven me mad by now."

"Hmm. So, when your research is done, you'll leave again?"

"I pretty much hitchhiked in, and I'll do the same when I've learned all I want. The Robokind will probably take me most of the way back to friendly space, as long as I keep being nice to them. I find them quite hard to get on with sometimes, to be honest, always so wrapped up in their own communities, whining to anyone who'll listen about the angst of being disconnected from their big, collective minds on other worlds… but they can be useful allies."

"I see."

"But you've only told me about your home, not how you came to be here. Carry on with your tale."

Matthias took a deep breath. "Yeah, Lambda Aurigae. I lived there for many years in much the same way as my family and friends. I studied art, literature, mathematics, got involved in some geothermal engineering projects on some of the inner asteroids, all the respectable things that were expected of me. One day I just fancied a break, so I enrolled in a programme to study developing alien cultures, because it seemed interesting and an excuse to finally leave the system. I didn't think I'd actually be accepted; I didn't think I was any better qualified than the other applicants, but perhaps I just got lucky. I was put on a survey ship with about five hundred others to go and look at a pre-industrial culture we'd detected in one of the neighbouring systems."

Sonja, still looking for a spoon, opened a drawer, having presumably exhausted all the kitchen's cutlery hiding-places. She recoiled in surprise, spilling some of the hot water on the towel. It took Matthias a few moments to remember what was in the drawer which might have surprised her.

"Oh, that's plastissue."

"I'm… sorry, I didn't mean to jump, it's just such a long time since I've seen any."

"It's all I managed to rescue from my ship. I mean, besides what I used for making my body shell. I wasn't sure what to do with it, so I kept it for… spare, I suppose. Y'know, if I fancy having a replacement hand or something."

"You're not worried about any humans finding it?"

"Not really. I doubt they'd be that freaked if they did see it, I could just tell them I like collecting sausage meat. Stranger things happen, especially in this country."

She laughed. “Or, if you wanted, you could make a pet from it. There must be enough there for a cat or a poodle.”

“That too. I like to keep my options open.” He grinned, but it soon faded. The story had to continue.

“Anyway… we spent several planetary years investigating that world, mostly just observing and cataloguing stuff from high orbit; you know how it is with our non-interventionist policies. Occasionally we’d send parties down to the surface, but only in remote spots where we wouldn’t be seen; pick a botanical sample here, exhume a grave there. The planet was a little bit smaller than this one and had two sentient races emerging at more or less the same time, which made it quite unique. Both carbon-based and oxygen breathing, one lot were amphibious and the other were land creatures, not that different from humans in some respects.

“It was fascinating stuff; like you’d expect, there were skirmishes between the two cultures, but not all-out warfare. In fact, we observed a lot of trade going on between them; the land-based creatures were able to manufacture metals goods which required fire, for instance, which they’d often barter with the amphibians for fish or minerals extracted from sea vents. We were in the later stages of our studies there, and already had enough data to keep scholars busy for centuries, when we detected an interstellar dust cloud approaching the system. The native races didn’t have any astronomy to speak of and they didn’t know what was about to happen, but we realised within a few years it would block out all the light from their star and cause mass extinctions on their world.”

Sonja, having finally located a spoon and wiped it clean on her towel, returned to bed to drink it. “That’s terrible,” she whispered.

“We’d not gone in there expecting this sort of crisis; we were light years from civilisation and couldn’t call for assistance, so of course we wasted a lot of valuable time debating what we should do. Our ship was big, but there was no way it could effectively lift out more than a couple of thousand specimens and, even then, it wasn’t properly fitted out to accommodate those forms of life. Some thought we should leave them to their fate, because once we’d involved ourselves in their affairs, their cultural development was permanently fucked anyway. Some of us argued we should still lift some specimens out, back off to a safe distance and wait a few years until the dust cloud had passed, then try and reintroduce them to the surface of their world, if it was still habitable at all. Others still thought we should just grab as many as we could and take them back home for resettlement in a specially built habitat we could somehow knock together, perhaps inside an asteroid or somewhere.”

Sonja sat listening intently. She looked very serious now and, despite the warmth of the afternoon, she had now retreated back under the duvet and sat with it gathered around her.

“Personally, I wasn’t too bothered whether we took specimens to another home, or just kept them onboard the ship until the dust cloud had passed by, but I just wanted to make sure some were rescued. But then, there were further problems because, as I said, the ship wasn’t fitted out for such passengers, especially for keeping them onboard for long periods. The crew was meant to consist only of Diagrax, so it was all aquatic chambers. We could retrofit some areas for the amphibious species, but trying to get the other race onboard at short notice was really going to cause problems for our engineers.

“Finally, when the cloud was already engulfing the mother star and the planets were beginning to freeze, we sent down a landing party to try and round up as many creatures as we could take. There was no time to build camouflaged body shells for us all, so we just had to set the ship down and march out in our pressurised armour suits. As I'm sure you can imagine, it scared the living shit out of the natives… probably when they saw us, they assumed we were responsible for dimming their sun too. I was in the middle of a desert with a couple of the others, trying to catch the land bipeds… a very difficult task, considering I wasn't used to the gravity and the armour suits weren't designed for catching delicate living things which clearly didn't want to be caught. They'd told us an oxygen enclosure on the ship was being drained of water and refitted to give them a more comfortable ride.

"We had four of the natives struggling to escape from a big cage, dragging the thing back to our shuttle, when news comes in that the sea-dwellers are considered better candidates for long-term survival and the dry enclosure would be re-flooded immediately." Matthias paused now. He looked at Sonja to ensure she wasn't falling asleep; she reached out and touched his hand. "Have you ever visited the zoo here?"

"Many times."

"Well, I'm sure you can imagine how the keepers there would react if the managers just decided one day to flood the lion pens. I'd been tracking various individuals of this race remotely for a few of the local years and, even though they might not have known my face, I'd sure as hell got attached to them. And we were talking about the extinction of an entire species – sure, the dust cloud was a tragedy not of our making, but what gave us the right to decide some couldn't have a chance to survive? I didn't honestly see how having both lots on our ship would significantly alter their long-term survival chances. But our so-called experts decided, if we were going to establish a new breeding colony, then they'd need as broad a gene pool as possible to ensure their long-term survival, so we were just going to fill up the ship with the stronger of the two races."

"And what did you do?"

"Went berserk, that's what I did. I mean, nobody was happy of course, but the rest of my team just started freeing the specimens from the cage and heading back to the shuttle, like they wanted to get the whole thing over with quickly and not have to think about the implications."

"And what happened then?"

"To cut to the chase, Sonja, I killed two of my own kind."

Her face froze in horror. "You're… *Serious*?"

"Totally. Regardless of how futile it was, I tried to physically stop the members of my team from abandoning the native creatures. A fight ensued and, when you're wearing powered armour and they aren't expecting violence and… I don't know, I think humans call it *the red mist*. I had the equivalent of that."

"My god."

"Indeed. I think some of the natives died of fright watching the whole incident unfold, too. Poor bastards. I got thrown in solitary confinement for the remainder of the mission - that was a very long time, by the way - because nobody knew what else to do with me. And the mission failed, too. Not only was all life on that planet eradicated, but when the amphibians and a few other minor species were re-introduced years later, the whole attempt at re-starting the ecosystem failed miserably. The food chains wouldn't re-establish themselves, no matter what we did – probably not enough biodiversity survived, or we overlooked some important plankton or soil microbes – and everything was extinct within a decade."

Sonja had nothing to comment on this. Her face twitched slightly as she fought to suppress certain emotions. Her mouth opened and closed a couple of times before words finally formed again: "You didn't see another soul for years, while all this was going on?"

"Very infrequently. It would be a bit of an understatement to say I had time to reflect on what I did. It would also be true to say I went a bit 'funny in the head,' as they say here. But in some respects it wasn't much worse than a long, solitary space journey. In any case, I had plenty of time to get over it."

"And what happened when you returned home?"

"They had no better idea what to do with me than the crew on my ship did. They did all sorts of behavioural tests and didn't think I posed a threat to society, but they couldn't just let me go as if nothing had happened; I think there was some ancient, unfulfilled need for retribution from the families of the deceased and what have you. They didn't spell it out to me, but it was obvious I wouldn't find life easy or comfortable if I stayed in the Lambda Aurigae system. I didn't have that many affairs to tie up anyway, so I didn't hang around there for long; I left again in a single-seat craft, heading further down the Perseus Arm, away from our people. I think you know the rest of the tale."

"I have to say," Sonja replied slowly and with care, "that isn't what I'd been expecting to hear."

VIII

14.231.785-2

While Matthias had never grown fully accustomed to the striking colour of Earth's sky, he mourned the passing of the summer blue and the gradual fade to grey. He sat alone in the Weinberg park, listening to the distant rumble of traffic beyond the trees and watching the miniature dust devils swirl over the parched, balding grass. He rubbed his eyes to remove bits of grit and shivered. Autumn would soon turn wet and the grass would have a short while to re-establish itself before everything froze. It would be many months before human backsides returned to wear the greenness away. In Iraq, the Americans were still searching for Saddam Hussein. In London, David Blaine was attracting media attention by sealing himself inside a perspex cube for weeks without any food. An old man walked his dog in the distance, but otherwise the park was his alone. It no longer held any interest; he stood up and began to trudge back to his apartment, through the children's area and past the now silent fountains.

The last few weeks had been uneventful. He'd had very little contact with the Book Club, or Sonja. His attempts at curing Bernhard's ageing had all failed, and now much of the equipment which had cluttered his apartment was either packed away, disposed of, or collecting dust. Bernhard had taken the news well enough, but then it had hardly been a shock. A short while after Sonja had stayed the night, the group had summoned him back to Simone's place, where they'd asked him to erase Torsten's memory. Matthias hadn't spent much time wondering why they might have chosen him in particular for this task; they told him it was because he'd shown himself to be most adept with human biology, but he thought it more likely they felt uncomfortable about performing a brain-wipe (a small murder, of sorts) and the revelation about his own past had made him the strongest candidate to perform the operation.

Since his episode at the party, Torsten had been sedated and locked in one of Simone's closets. Some investigations had revealed a father and a sister living in Bremen, although he didn't seem to have communicated with them in a couple of years and he'd more recently been taking a cocktail of medication for depression. Dylan had theorised he'd also suffered some kind of mental breakdown shortly prior to meeting the Book Club, possibly after losing his last job, and for him the divide between reality and fantasy had become dangerously thin. It had been tempting to merely brainwash him into thinking what he'd seen was imaginary, but that presented too many dangers for the future, if Torsten were to come back looking for the group to try and reconcile his corrupted memories. No, the only safe option was the total eradication of his neural pathways which stored the knowledge of what he'd seen and heard and Matthias had reached into the man's skull and quietly, dispassionately, taken out a few grams of tissue. Torsten had regained consciousness, confused but apparently still relatively himself. He'd have very little recollection of the last two years and Simone had walked him to the train station with a case full of clothes and money and a pre-booked ticket to Bremen.

There had been some recriminations towards Bernhard and other members of the group who claimed they were able to 'sniff out' out aliens from other races. There was no excuse offered for letting Torsten slip through undetected, other than that *some species have stronger smells than others and how were we to know what a 'Nitid' smells like?*

And that had been that. He'd kept hold of the business card, and a scrap of paper with Sonja's own number written on it, but there was a feeling that he had nothing more to say to any of them. They didn't call him either and he half-consciously avoided the streets near to Simone's apartment or the dimly lit bar near Alexanderplatz, as he no longer knew how he should greet any of them. His body shell was capable of growing a beard, and he had considered giving this a try at one point, but then dismissed the idea, deciding it would look too obviously like he was trying to hide himself, and that implied he was ashamed. Besides, it would hardly suit his face – by now more familiar in the mirror – and the others could probably still located him if they really wanted to anyway.

He'd contented himself with human affairs, which had been his main goal for living in Berlin anyway. For the most part this had been positive, although an apartment on the floor beneath his was burgled and, fearing that some of the more sensitive alien objects in his home might be discovered, he took to carrying them around on his person whenever he left the place unoccupied. Reading through mountains of human literature had brought some unexpected rewards, as had a thorough exploration of the city's galleries and museums. He'd been to the opera and stood beneath the unblinking marble gaze of Greek statues at the Pergamon, which he estimated must have been chiselled by long-dead craftsmen around the same time he was a mewling infant in the artificial ocean of a fake planet, too far away for the astronomers of the day to have guessed at. Television at first seemed crass and unstimulating, but gradually he learned his way around the schedules, investing in a bigger set and making time to settle down and watch certain items. The government had not long ago decriminalised brothels, but he felt little compulsion to try them. He already knew more than he wished to about human coupling and saw little point in imposing this on another just because he had the money and time for it. As he slowly forgot about his night with Sonja, so too did his need for sleep dissipate, and once again he had the whole period of earth's rotation to do with as he liked. He frequented more and more cinemas, restaurants and bars and familiarised himself with more of the Western world's popular and not-so-popular subcultures. He spotted the Englishman again on one occasion, who smiled and nodded wanly, before mingling back into the crowd. Several other familiar faces paraded past in a succession of different locations. For a short while, he left Germany and flew to Paris, London and Rome, though he found all cities to be variations on the same themes and decided to cancel further planned trips to America, Russia and China. There would be nothing to learn there. Matthias was actually coming to envy Bernhard – at least Bernhard would die before he had fully used up the planet's ability to entertain.

The chill from sitting down had still not quite gone and Matthias quickened his pace to try and stave off the cold as he headed down Kastanienalle away from the park. Once he'd had a chance to extract more money from an ATM, a thick coat would have to be one of the first things to buy with it. As he hurried past a Lebanese restaurant, there came a knocking on one of the windows from within. He paused in mid-step, wondering who was trying to get his attention. The restaurant was dark inside and the glass reflected back only his own likeness. Was it somebody of importance, or just some crank who was worth avoiding? There were certainly enough of those around, even within the human community. As he stood there between decisions, Thomas appeared at the doorway.

hargh "Matthias!"

"Oh, hi there, I didn't recognise you for a moment."

"When did you get back from Zürich?"

"Oh, only yesterday. In the evening."

"It's so good to see you again! I'm on early shifts at the factory this week, it's great, now I have all afternoon to drink and chill out. Come on in, meet my friends, have a drink. They've got some great lamb and falafel in here, oh and the couscous… I tried to look you up in the phonebook and online, but I couldn't seem to reach you."

"Really? Well, look Thomas, maybe we could catch up properly some time when I've—"

"Oh no, no, you must come in and talk to us now! I've been doing so much work on my writing, you're going to love this, really." Before Matthias could think up a proper excuse, Thomas had already placed his hand on his shoulder and was directing him towards the door.

"You've still got your cough?"

"Huh? Oh, yes."

"What is this?" Matthias asked, confused, as he handled the dog-eared pages of laser printed manuscript. "I thought you were trying to write a novel?"

"Not any more." Thomas's eyes shone, reflecting the hundreds of small Christmas tree lights which seemed to be the restaurant's main illumination. "It's my very first screenplay! I finished it – the first draft, I mean – about a week ago. Do you want a beer?"

"Not rea—"

Thomas flagged down the waiter and ordered another round of beers. "I just need to iron out a few little plot holes and improve some of the dialogue, then I think this could have Hollywood potential. Olga," he paused, indicating the vaguely hippy-looking woman next to him with dreadlocks and baggy wool sweater, "Olga speaks good English, she's going to translate it for me. For *us*."

As his eyes slowly adjusted to the low light, Matthias scanned page after page of text. The first act of the movie, as far as he could make out, was a fairly accurate depiction of life in his home system, as he'd explained it to Thomas three months earlier, albeit peopled with typically humanoid creatures. The following plot seemed like conventional Hollywood fare, with a renegade running from his people and being shot out of the Earth's sky by a fighter jet, where he is then forced to integrate with human society. Some clinking across the table indicated that the beers had arrived.

"If I'd known I'd run into you again, I'd have brought a spare copy with me," Thomas sighed. "But there's a stationers down the road from here, perhaps they can run one off for you."

"No, it's okay, really. So how does your story conclude?"

"The alien visitor is pursued by agents of his own people and also the FBI, but he knows he has to retrieve a crystal which was lost on Earth centuries ago by his people, and that alone can avert a terrible war."

Matthias examined his unwanted beer and took a sip. "Right. Well… why not? Good luck with that."

"I'd really like you to be a script consultant on this project."

Matthias was about to say, "So it's a project now?" but checked himself. "And everything ends happily for the galaxy?" He asked, instead.

"Eventually, yes. He gets the girl, he builds a new ship and escapes from Earth, it's a real classic action narrative."

"He builds a new ship?"

"Oh, sure. I still need to flesh out some details about how he's going to do that, but he's a—" *hargh hargh hargh* "--an engineering genius, so anything's possible."

Matthias took a long swig of the beer while trying to project the look that he was seriously considering the idea.

"And, I know it's not actually gone to a studio or an agent yet, or anything, so we shouldn't be counting our chickens as it were, but I've intentionally left the end open, in case we want to, you know, develop it as a franchise. What does our hero – I've called him Daniel, by the way – do next? Does he return to Earth? There's all sorts of subplots we could write in, the romantic one being the most obvious, but there's other stuff too. Robots and cyborgs infiltrating the human population in disguise, sinister creatures from other dimensions pulling the strings of the interstellar conflict. Hey, this is science fiction, anything's possible."

* * * *

Matthias cursed the cold again as he continued down Kastanienalle, then Zionskirche Straße. Waiting by the kerb for a break in the traffic so he could cross, he hugged himself to stave off another icy gust of wind and cursed the fact that his bladder was now approaching full, mocking his other discomforts. He took the crumpled slip of paper from his pocket, on which Thomas had scribbled his name, address, email, landline and cell numbers. Damn this miserable little planet, he'd had enough of it now.

What had Bernhard said at that party, during the summer? Create a pandemic by releasing unknown bacterial cultures into the Earth's environment. Hah, what a typically narrow-minded Cephalic idea. The humans had reached that point in their development when they suspected the existence of so much but did not yet possess the experience, the intellect or the patience to grasp these things. How much more infinitely destructive it would be to hand them these sciences now, while they are so eager but so ill-prepared for them. How interesting that would be for anthropology; nobody that he knew of in galactic history had ever tried such a grotesque experiment. Holding all the cards, he would be hailed as the greatest celebrity of this world, with the human's desire for new technology safely counterbalancing any want for dissecting him in a laboratory. In fact, he could ask their governments to build him a new starship and they'd probably do it.

He wouldn't do any of that, of course. Even if he could escape, the repercussions would be slow but terrible for doing things that way. No, the future instead looked like it held phone calls from Thomas. But something was now tugging at the back of his mind, and it was not the human writer. Something else had just surfaced in his memory and was bobbing close to the surface… something else to do with Bernhard?

And suddenly, there it was.

IX

14.231.785-4

A short U-Bahn trip later, Matthias walked briskly, immune to the cold now, along the street where he remembered Simone lived. He remained a little nervous about running into one of the Book Club people again, but now he felt charged with renewed purpose and, at least for the moment until he calmed down, he didn't much care.

"Skirr doesn't get out much nowadays," Bernhard had said.

Matthias stopped by the front door to the block, with its chunky, ornate woodwork and peeling, graffiti-streaked paint. A lot of people must come and go during the day, making deliveries perhaps, or maybe the lock was just broken, because it now stood ajar and he could walk through the hallway with its parked bicycles and rows of mail boxes, to the small, square courtyard at the centre of the building.

He stood now in the courtyard, seeing little but recycling bins, more bicycles, graffiti tags and brambles which grew from between the paving stones. He'd not looked out of Simone's living room window when he'd called before, but he suspected if she happened to be looking from it right now, she'd likely be able to see him. He had to move quickly, and hope the old lady had more pressing matters to divert her attention.

This might, of course, be a wild goose chase. Skirr might not be in the city at all… but if he had something to hide, something so unlikely, yet so explosively dangerous if it were ever found… With the aid of his memory bionics, he had retained a fairly accurate map of Simone's apartment and felt satisfied he wouldn't find what he was looking for in there. There simply wasn't enough free space unaccounted for, not to mention the difficulty of negotiating all the stairs to her front door. But— His heart froze when he glanced back up at her window and noticed, for the first time, a small device fixed to a bracket just underneath the ledge. A miniature CCTV camera, the kind available from home improvement stores, pointing right at the spot where he stood. Was there any point in even trying to run?

It was possible the camera was set up for live monitoring of the courtyard only, without the facility to record. Maybe it was simply a dummy, put there to deter burglars, but he couldn't take that for granted; without knowing what the camera was connected to, he had to assume evidence of his visit had already been stored. Sure, perhaps no-one spared the time to examine the recording unless given a good reason and, in days or weeks, his image would eventually get erased or re-recorded over. Yes, he decided. If I leave now and return in, say, a month, perhaps with a hooded top or a disguise, then my visit today would not matter… But another question presented itself, as he turned to leave: why have a camera there? There was none by the front door to the building, or on the landing outside Simone's apartment, which would seem the obvious places for them. Was she paranoid about someone stealing the recycling?

He turned to face the wall behind the bins, in the direct sight of the little lens. The bottom six feet of the wall looked like it had been re-plastered hastily, at a more recent time than the rest of the building. On this side of the courtyard there was only a single, small window close to the ground, and that was covered up from the inside by yellowed old pages from newspapers. At first glance he'd thought nothing of this, since the old East German government had been notoriously slipshod in a lot of its civic restoration projects, and this wall probably covered nothing more interesting than a tool cupboard, where a superintendent went to read dirty magazines. But there was an easy way to find out.

Squeezing past one of the bins, he found a small stairwell, made almost impassable by blown litter and weeds, leading down to an old wooden door, so warped by rain that it seemed unlikely to move. He carefully traversed the steps and rotated the door handle, as quietly as he could but, unsurprisingly, it was locked. It didn't look like a very sophisticated lock and Matthias knew in theory how it might be picked, but that hardly mattered right now, without the correct tools or any prior hands-on experience. He took a deep breath. Go away, acquire the tools and equipment, then return in a month or more and hope they wouldn't be expecting him? If he did, would he open the door only to find more alarms or traps waiting on the other side? There was a faint, odd smell coming from the other side of the door. It was difficult to place and probably wouldn't have made a native suspicious, but the smell seemed strangely out of place here.

Placing one foot against the door frame and bracing his back against the damp wall inside the stairwell, he grasped the handle with both hands and began to pull. Most humans wouldn't have the strength to do this, but by forcing more oxidised molecules through the muscle cells in his body shell, it was possible to achieve a momentary burst of abnormal strength - he just had to hope the wood of the door would break first, and not the handle. There were a series of short groans and cracks, then a small explosion of splinters, as a chunk of the door came away in his hand, leaving a hole where the lock had been. The darkness beyond seemed to shine outwards and he wasted no time in putting his arm through and heaving the damp and swollen wood panelling aside.

The smell was stronger within and there wasn't enough light filtering through the newsprint-covered window or down through the stairwell to properly illuminate what was inside. Matthias fumbled for a light switch and eventually turned on a single, bare low-wattage bulb in one corner. The room was part of a small, sparsely furnished bed-sit; or at least what had once been used as a bed-sit, some time ago. The source of the odour was immediately apparent: dominating the centre of the room was a living thing about a metre and a half in length and one in height and width, resembling what the head of a tyrannosaurus might look like if it were freshly removed and still had flesh attached. Most of the floor was still covered by an ornately patterned (and heavily stained) old carpet, but Matthias could see that the floor boards beneath it were bowed from the weight of this huge thing. It emitted a faintly audible, laboured breathing sound and the exhalations were just strong enough to make the fabric of his clothes flutter. The creatures eyes were closed and a number of narrow rubber tubes ran from IV points in its flesh to a pile of complicated-looking distillation equipment on top of a rusted old fridge.

Matthias cautiously placed a hand on its thick, leathery skin. He knew little about Cephalus physiology, but the creature seemed distinctly ill. This probably explained the odour; no human would have recognised this reek of decay, because they knew nothing of alien biochemistry.

"Skirr? You're Skirr, aren't you?"

Two of the tennis ball-sized eyes opened a little, very slowly. They were the colour of glowing coals, shot through with hundreds of intricate veins and with tar black centres. They adjusted slowly to the surroundings and focused in on Matthias. The creature exhaled loudly, momentarily parting its huge lips to reveal rows of dagger-like teeth, although it was doubtful if the creature had enough strength to open its huge jaw. First came a faint rattle, then it emitted a long and ululating moan.

"I'm sorry, I can't understand that. Do you have a translation box anywhere?"

Another moan.

“Do you understand anything I’m saying? Make two noises?”

This time there was no response; this wasn’t going to be at all easy. Something small, grey and roughly cylindrical emerged from a sphincter in the middle of the huge face. What was this? It was about the same size as a segment from a human little finger and it plinked to the floor with a sound which suggested it was quiet solid. Matthias stared at it, wondering if that was an important gesture, or simply an autonomous body function. He cursed his lack of knowledge of the species, although he could see no other such pellets lying around on the floor, so he surmised it was something Skirr wanted him to have.

“What’s this for?” Still feeling a little foolish, he smelt the object, which had an odour similar to broken polystyrene. Skirr made a faint moan.

He held it close to his mouth. ”Do I eat it?”

Another moan.

Nothing for it, then; with some difficulty, he swallowed the strange thing, which seemed more mineral than anything organic. Skirr remained silent.

Not sure what was meant to happen next, Matthias stood up and began examining the room for other clues as to how long the Cephalus had been imprisoned here. He knew that, on Cephalus worlds, they relied mainly on specially bred symbiotic scurrying creatures to transport their immobile forms around. These creatures had no minds of their own and were rarely carried on space missions. There didn’t seem to be any trace of them around this apartment, so Skirr must have been carried here by other means; probably lifted in through the wall and then had it bricked up again.

He felt a sharp prickling feeling from his stomach lining. The sensation faded, then came again, repeating itself with increasing vigour until he found breathing difficult. Hardly having any time to react, Matthias doubled up, wondering if he could retch up that grey pellet, but as suddenly as the pain had started it then stopped again. In his minds eye, fixed and unwavering, were thoughts which he knew were not his own. Ideas, memories and sensations expanded into view and contracted again – for a few moments, this was even more intolerable than the physical pain, until he got the hang of controlling the flood of new information. He had little doubt that he was seeing inside Skirr's mind. Was the pellet somehow allowing psychic communication between the two of them? A particular idea would collapse back into a vague impression once he'd finished examining it, and saw that an index of these ghostly thumbnails spread before him, from which he could select at will with a little practice. No, this was not real-time communication, it was a dump of old mental information. He had swallowed the biological equivalent of a USB memory stick… but there was far too much here to sift through at short notice. He would need to travel home and hope the information would not degrade in clarity as the pellet passed through his gut. Was there something particular in here which Skirr wanted him to have?

The Cephalus, watching him the whole time with its firey eyes, moaned softly and a particular series of impressions – he could think of them now almost like icons on a human PC desktop – expanded by themselves to fill his consciousness. He saw a crudely constructed three-dimensional map of the building, with two hidden rooms, one ahead and one beneath. Clearly, these contained things of interest and would need exploring.

This idea now collapsed and another took its place in the sequence. This was not a thought so much as an experience; through another being's eyes, he witnessed a long flight in suspended animation within the safe womb-like surroundings of a capsule; a technical failure which necessitated finding a suitable nearby world with an oxygen atmosphere; making contact with any other offworlders on Earth who would offer aid, terrified that human would locate the capsule first; some members of the Book Club (Simone's inner circle, perhaps? He noted there were no Robokind among them) entering the apartment and adjusting the apparatus, placing morsels of human food in his mouth - and, to a Cephalus palette, these tasted foul. They spoke to him in tongues he could not understand, even Bernhard did, and they poked and prodded the tender areas of his body where disease was starting to take hold. On a couple of occasions they slapped or punched him in frustration, although the reason for their anger seemed more and more unclear with the passage of time. Matthias felt this memory must be temporally disjointed, because he must be seeing events which took place over a number of months or years, but it was impossible to tell for certain. Lucid periods were punctuated by long, confused lapses of confusion and drowsiness, which intensified with time as the diseases spread throughout his immobile body. It became impossible to even tell how long he'd been 'watching' this scene for, such was the feeling of timelessness it pressed upon him as the recipient. Only the growing despair acted as a metronome against the passing jumble of experiences in this room. One certainty remained when the memory dribbled to an end: Skirr wanted nothing more than to die.

With some effort, he was able to close the memories down and push them away to the back of his conscious mind, where they faded from view. Spurred on by the mental map of the building, he pulled aside a drape with a psychedelic tie-dye print, to reveal the top of a doorway, blocked by a chest of drawers. Pulling this away, he opened the door to the tiny bathroom, and immediately recoiled in horror. There was a human inside, crouching in the shadows, and a powerful smell, more familiar and overpowering than the Cephalus, billowed out to greet him. He was about to slam it again, but the figure hardly moved, except to tremble in fear. A bloodshot eye glared at him for a few moments, then a hand moved to cover it. The man scrawny was naked and filthy from head to toe, with sores and half-healed cuts at seemingly random points on his body; had he inflicted these on himself? Trying to hold his breath against the stench, Matthias located the light cord; a number of empty bowls and food packets littered the floor and there was excrement smeared on the walls.

"Torsten?"

The man sobbed quietly to himself.

"Torsten, what are you doing here? How long have they been keeping you down here?"

"I—I'm so sorry. I'm sorry." Torsten rocked back forth, still clutching himself for warmth and protection.

"Why are you sorry?"

"Sorry. Sorry. Sorry."

Breathing through his mouth in a futile attempt to ignore the fetid air, Matthias searched the room for any useful objects, while Torsten flinched away whenever he came too close. There was a small wooden medical chest, secured with a dainty padlock, which he forced open by hand. Inside, among the normal bog standard first aid dressings, tools and ointments, were some phials of what might be morphine and a couple of syringes, which he pocketed.

"Look, I'm going to try and get you some help, okay? I should have done that before, but I definitely will now. You just hang on in there."

Just as soon as I can figure out how, without any humans coming down here and seeing the rest of this stuff, he thought. Moving slowly to avoid further startling him, Matthias switched off the light and closed the bathroom door, moving the chest back into place in front of it; if any of the others realised he'd seen Torsten, that could further endanger him.

What to do with the Cephalus? What substance here – if anything – might serve to send it painlessly into oblivion? It would have to be the morphine. Filling the syringe's chamber, as best he could with trembling hands, he supposed that anything so alien to the creature would have a violent reaction with its metabolism, especially in its present weakened state. He just hoped it would at least have a sedative or euphoric effect as it went to work. Locating a vein near the surface, he pushed the needle through leathery skin and depressed the plunger. Wiping away a tear, he watched one of the big eyes slowly start to dilate and the breathing pattern alter. For the second time in his existence, Matthias was a killer, but whether or not that altered anything he couldn't guess. He would have some time ahead to contemplate that.

He had to steal his gaze away, it was too much. Almost too frightened now to look anywhere else, not knowing what else to expect to see, but if he was to be able to deal with any of this, he had to know the full extent of what the Book Club was hiding. There was one final place to look; the edge of a trapdoor was visible where one side of the carpet ended. It looked like it hadn't been opened for some time, judging by the way the carpet, stiff with congealed alien fluids and thick with dust, was laid over the top of it. With difficulty, he managed to roll it back far enough to see that the wooden hatch was not padlocked. He tugged it open and strained his eyes into the cold, musty smelling void beneath. Something was faintly reflecting the electric light from above. Cursing himself for not bringing a torch, Matthias descended a couple of the crumbling cement steps and cautiously extended his hand. It didn't go far before making contact with a smooth metal surface. He traced its curving shape an arms length in all directions, then a bit more… the bulbous object was roughly teardrop shaped and two or three metres in diameter. Christ, he thought, don't let that be a bomb from the last war. Even during the short time he'd lived in Berlin, two main roads had been evacuated due to workers unearthing ancient British devices. But no, the surface was too well preserved; those old weapons weren't built to last and even in a stable environment it would be almost too corroded by now to hold its shape. This was something else entirely and it cast significant doubt on going to the human authorities for help – they mustn't see this at any cost. As his eyes slowly adjusted, he saw that some rock and earth had been hewn from the floor of the cellar in order to accommodate this thing.

His attention now turned to the collection of jars and tubes which were connected to the Cephalus. The bizarre apparatus seemed to have been assembled from a mixture of scavenged hospital supplies and home wine-making equipment and his initial impression, that this was some sort of dialysis rig, seemed to be correct. After passing through a number of chambers, something was being extracted from the rest of the fluid and stored in a large glass vessel, while the rest was passed back into circulation. The waste product – if such it was – looked familiar. Matthias tilted it slightly, this way and that, watching the viscous amber fluid move around. Another wave of revulsion sprung up in the pit of his stomach; of course he knew what this was, he'd drunk some at that party.

"Matthias," said a voice behind him. "I'm very disappointed, if a little unsurprised, to see you couldn't keep your nose out."

He turned and found himself face to face with Simone. How long had it taken her to hobble all the way down the stairs from her apartment? he wondered. Probably she'd seen him as he first entered the courtyard. "Nice place you have here," he answered. "Is this your guest house?"

"This place is none of your business. I thought the lock on the door should have made that obvious. I've called all the others and they're on their way here, so don't even think of trying anything."

"That's nice. Thank you, Simone. I'm a little confused that you people could shun me for having killed one of my own, and yet you're content to do this."

She scowled at him. "Don't you dare pass judgment on us! What you did may not have been premeditated, but it was an act of unforgivable – and un*necessary* barbarism. This may not be tasteful to you, and perhaps it would be to me also, if I were a newcomer to Earth, but I'm afraid you need a serious reality lesson in surviving here."

"A lesson you felt it necessary to hide from me?"

"You weren't exactly forthcoming about your murderous past, either."

"Touché. So, does Bernhard know what you're doing to one of his people down here?"

"Bernhard is very well aware and I've summoned him along with all the others. He will doubtless be unhappy to find you here." Simone forced the warped old door closed, as best she could, and seated herself on a wooden stall. "You know we would have happily shared our community with you, and all of its benefits, had you been more forthright with us from the start, and if you could – ironic though I find this – put aside some of your more naïve ideas. Look at this bloody planet. Have you learned nothing while you've been here? They're infants, no more than a couple of generations out of savagery. Yes, some of us came to this world by choice, but even they will happily tell you how sick they've become of it, after a stay of only a few short Earth years. We've made a tiny, precious oasis of true civilisation here for ourselves, where we can temporarily shut out the horrors of humanity, and if we have to…" she surveyed the interior of the room with a hint of sadness. "The humans themselves have a saying, *you can't make an omelette without breaking some eggs*.

"Skirr was forced to ditch here when the control systems in his capsule failed. By great fortune, we found him before the humans did, but how exactly would you hide a creature like this? Bernhard may be trapped in a body that's rapidly aging, but at the very least he's free to roam undetected on this planet. Skirr was always going to be denied that and – it may surprise you to learn – he *chose this*. We don't kill our own, Matthias."

He groped for those memories once more, to see if Skirr's thoughts could be dragged back onto the plane of his conscious. Fortunately, yes, there they were, obediently returning to centre stage in his mind. Hastily, Matthias searched them for information on Skirr's ship.

"You've near enough killed Torsten."

"Ah. So you did look in the bathroom. Yes, poor Torsten. Like any of his kind, he allowed himself to be ruled by curiosity and wild flights of imagination. Even after you'd so kindly purged us from his little brain, he came back in search of his missing past. Such a tenacious thing. Perhaps, as you're qualified in ending lives, you'd do us all the honour of capping his suffering?"

He had suspected that was coming, but it still made Matthias feel sick to the pit of his stomach. He wondered how long he had before the others started to show up, and whether they would imprison him here too. He couldn't really imagine doing anything else, if he were in their position. "You aren't interested in civilisation," he indicated the distillery in the corner. “What’s all that? No matter how bad you might find life here, it’s a bad joke to call *that* an oasis of culture.”

She moved protectively in front of the equipment. “That’s where you’re wrong. You’re no expert on Cephalus chemistry,” she looked at Skirr for a moment, hopefully assuming that his closed, inert eyes merely indicated sleep. How long, Matthias wondered, until she noticed he wasn’t breathing?

“We’re not just producing drugs for our own gratification. Oh no, there is a grand scheme in place here, which I’d have happily explained to you under better circumstances.”

“Please do now, it all looks so nice.”

“What you tasted in my home was nectar at its first stage of refinement. The first of many; in its crudest form yes, it is a catalyst for dopamine release, and other pleasure reactions, depending on the user’s brain. But when it’s been refined and stripped of all its simpler protein molecules it becomes a potent drug for boosting intelligence. Not only that, but it’s mutagenic; so future generations of the user will also benefit from increased mental power.

“With such a small plant, of course, production’s painfully slow, so it’s not as if we could dump it in a drinking reservoir and enlighten the whole world overnight, but we occasionally target select individual humans, when we think it might bring particular rewards. A drop in the ocean, I suppose, but it must be helping Earth a bit. And it helps us, when we need to have regular contact with those people too – we call it social terraforming.”

“That goes against every rule my people – and yours too, I’m sure – have for the treatment of developing—“

“Spare me any more lectures. Who’s ever going to know? Or really, honestly, care? Get a sense of perspective.”

A shadow moved on the paper covering the window. Whatever he planned to do, Matthias knew it had to be now. He leapt into the open hatch in the floor, landing painfully in the small hollow space afforded by the space capsule. His fingers groped in the darkness, feeling their way over the cold surface of its skin, looking for a release mechanism.

"What the hell are you doing?" Simone's voice continued to croak from the room above. "You won't benefit by messing with that. Stop being an arse and get back up here." A loud rasp indicated the front door had opened. The floorboards creaked and a hushed voice, probably Bernhard's conversed with Simone.

His fingers continued to search for a feature to grip. This thing definitely had a door somewhere, and it only made sense that they'd put the capsule in the cellar with the door facing the steps.

"Come on, get the hell out," shouted Bernhard, "let's not turn this any uglier."

His finger snagged a small indent and Matthias almost allowed himself a sigh of relief. A careful turn and the door raised itself out from the surface of the hull. Old mechanisms hissed back into life and slid it away to one side and violet lamps glowed dimly inside the cramped, stale space within. Matthias climbed inside, pulling in his legs and crouching on a strangely-shaped control couch, to re-seal the door against his pursuers. Only a being without proper limbs of its own could possibly endure even a short journey in this contraption. He began running his hands over the control displays and frantically flipped through experiences in the memory pellet for clues as to what to do next. Some screens lit up with streams of complicated glyphs, but there couldn't possibly be enough time to decipher what they meant.

There was a loud thump and a muffled shout outside of the ship. He hoped he'd locked the door correctly but, even if it were secured, he couldn't tell how long it might protect him from an attack. Another, deeper shouting voice indicated that Dylan had also turned up. A waving clump of tendrils extended from beneath the console; Matthias recoiled from it in horror, thinking some predatory creature had been placed in here as a sort of booby trap, but he relaxed when he realised it was the Cephalus equivalent of a joystick. Letting the tendrils wrap around his hands, he let his mind merge with that of the flight computer, looking for what needed to be repaired for takeoff.

"What's he trying to do in there?" Bernhard whispered. "He can't launch, the thing's way too damaged. Surely he'd have figured that out by now."

"He's getting desperate," Simone replied. "We've backed him into a hole. Partly my fault, I suppose; he's behaving like a cornered animal, so I say we back off for a bit and let him calm down. Otherwise there's no knowing what he might do next."

"Fuck that," Dylan growled, "he might be damaging the capsule. It might not be repairable now, but that doesn't mean it couldn't be a ticket home for one of us, one day. I'm not going to stand here and watch him trash it."

Simone nodded, sadly. "I don't want him hurting himself, either. Can you get him out of there with the least struggle possible?"

"I'll give it a shot, but that last part's up to him." Dylan climbed into the darkness and began to hammer on the door of the small craft. There were a few mechanical clunks, as he manually overrode the lock holding it closed and then the sound of a struggle which lasted for several painful seconds. Gathering around the hatch, Simone and Bernhard saw only Dylan's heaving back and an occasional flailing arm but then, as quickly as it had started, the struggle seemed to be over and the grunting was replaced by a faint, but steady hiss. With laboured breathing sounds, Dylan reappeared out of the cellar, his face strangely contorted, then he collapsed in a heap. With some difficulty, he rolled over, revealing a syringe protruding from his ribs and, a moment later, Matthias emerged from the cellar. The hiss continued, as if a very large amplifier were switched on, waiting for a voice or music to be be fed into it.

"Sorry about that. Had to dose him," Matthias explained, panting for breath, as he advanced towards Simone and Bernhard. Already, Dylan's abdomen had begun to swell and pulsate as something inside panicked to escape from within. "He might need a new body shell. I hope that one wasn't expensive."

14.231.785-5

Sonja rounded a corner onto Simone's street and half walked, half ran, threading her way through milling shoppers. She breathed raggedly, hoping that she wasn't too late. Skirting around a couple of mothers with pushchairs, she almost ran into a man walking a dachshund. She apologised awkwardly and was about to resume her hurry to Simone's apartment, when she did a double take, recognising the man.

"Matthias?"

"Hi Sonja."

When Simone had mentioned sending out an alarm call to the rest of her Book Club, he'd immediately wondered what sort of form that call might take; whether it contained any sort of specific message about the emergency, or if it was just some sort of generic ringing bell. Right now, he was praying through gritted teeth that it was the latter. Even if it is, he reasoned, she will probably see my presence here as suspicious.

"Matthias! What are you doing here?"

"Just walking the pooch, that's all. Sorry, are you in a rush? We can talk later, if you want. Or whatever."

She seemed to teeter between decisions for a moment. "No, it's nothing that important, I just, I just have to put some frozen food away before it melts. Over at Simone's. So, it's good to see you again. I'd been meaning to call you."

"You had?"

"Yeah, well it's been ages, hasn't it? You're looking well. I'm sorry things have been so awkward with us lately. Uhh, is that your dog?"

"Yeah, do you like him?"

"He's adorable. Is he… real?"

Matthias laughed. "You got me. No. I got bored of looking at that big lump of plastissue at my place, and I thought I could use some company. Did the nose give it away? Or the floppy ears – I think I may have made one of them slightly too short."

"No, he's just lovely." Sonja glanced over Matthias's shoulder, down the street towards Simone's apartment. "Look, we should really catch up properly some time, but I've got to be—"

"Well, let's talk now, then. Look, there's a café just over the street and there's indoor seating, why don't we grab something warm?"

"I really shouldn't, not this time—"

"Oh come on, your food won't thaw that quickly, especially in this weather." With one hand on her shoulder, he steered her across the street, narrowly avoiding a VW van, and towards the coffee bar, before she had time to think of another excuse to leave. The dachshund trotted silently and obediently at their heels. "His name's Lutz." Matthias added, cheerfully.

A waiter met them at the door to the café and explained that Lutz wasn't allowed inside, so they were redirected to a table on the street, warmed modestly by a battered porch heater. Matthias began to eagerly thumb through pages of the drinks menu.

"What's really going on here?"

"I'm sorry?"

“I don’t know what’s happening, but I think you’re trying to deceive me.”

Matthias held up his hands. He’d run out of delaying tactics. “Alright, look, if you have something important to do, then go.”

“Would you like to order?” Asked the waiter, reappearing behind them.

“I’ll have a regular black filter coffee please.” Matthias looked at Sonja expectantly.

“I’d better go.” She rose from her chair and shouldered her bag. “I’ll see you later some time.”

“Oh, okay. Bye then.”

She disappeared from view down the street and the waiter went back inside. Matthias took a deep breath as he collected his thoughts on what to do next. Well, the dog would have to go now. Checking that no passers by could see what he was doing, he reached under the table and pushed his fingers through the dachshund’s soft flanks and peeled away the flesh like he was peeling an orange.

“Oh, don’t look at me like that,” he whispered to it, seeing the puzzled expression in its eyes. He’d had no time to imbue the creature with a mind of its own, so instead it received a greatly simplified copy of his own personality. His fingers continued to dig until its entire torso had fallen away and the lumpy metallic rod at its core was exposed. He carefully pulled off the last bits of dog, which twitched aimlessly around on the ground for a few moments before lapsing back into their inanimate state. He cleaned the rod using the edge of the table cloth and stowed it carefully away in his rucksack; it was a miniaturised Cephalus antimatter reactor, possibly the most potentially destructive object on this entire planet, and he’d need to find something else to hide it inside before long. He wasn't sure how to dispose of the dachshund's remains, but resolved to tip the waiter generously when he'd finished his drink.

"Your coffee, sir."

"Thank you." Matthias idly eyed the tiny biscuit he'd also received on the edge of the coffee saucer when he felt a tremor run through the ground, followed by a sound like a thunderclap. Some crockery inside the café rattled a number of people yelped with alarm. "Did you feel that?"

The waiter nodded, looking a bit confused.

In his head, Matthias quickly retraced his journey here from Simone's flat. How long might it have taken Sonja to get there? Two minutes? Two and a half? He hoped she wouldn't have arrived; that maybe something else might have delayed her en route. She was most likely safe, but the uncertainty was unbearable. From above some of the rooftops across the road, a small mushroom cloud of black smoke now rolled into view. This was his own doing; he'd deliberately opened the spacecraft's dump valves while he pretended to be trying to fix its control systems. The whole basement flat would have flooded with hydrogen and it would have only taken one spark, perhaps from the refrigerator or a thermostat, to ignite the whole lot. An image passed through his mind of Sonja igniting it by walking in and pressing the light switch, but he suppressed it as best he could. She couldn't have got there already.

"Do you have a phone behind the bar?"

"Yes, sir. I'll call the Feuerwehr, right away."

"Good man."

Matthias stood up, left a fistful of Euros on the table – he hoped not to need them for much longer – turned, and left. He occasionally looked over his shoulder to see if he was being followed. He thought of the security camera overlooking the courtyard. Would anyone examine that footage? Maybe, but by then it would be too late. Sirens and horns began to blare ahead of him and soon a procession of fire engines and Polizei vans roared past in a stream of flickering blue light. Nobody paid him any attention.

Epilogue

14.324.199-5

One of the suns of Groombridge 34 shone dimly through a break in the marching cloud cover. The second sun was mostly hidden from view at this time in the year, eclipsed by the grey/beige bulk of a gas giant world, which forever filled a quarter of this world's sky with its own mottled jumble of band and chevron-shaped cloud formations.

Matthias was fascinated by this scenery, almost as much as by the bustle of daily life going on below it, but he made himself focus his eye stalks on the conversation in hand, not wishing to look like too much of a tourist. The dominant local species strode about precariously on their stilt-like legs, redundant leathery wings folded around their bodies to fend off the icy winds from the south. There had been a lot of volcanic activity in the last month, brought on by the close pass of another major moon, and a dark rain of ash was blowing across from over the horizon. A couple of small Robokind skimmers took off and headed for the safety of a low orbit. All around them, the inhabitants of the small settlement were closing shuttered windows and erecting sheets of tough fabric to deflect the storm.

Yakktranathac swivelled her own stalks to follow Matthias's curious gaze for a few moments then returned her attention to stirring a bowl of steaming, bitter soup. Her feeding tubes twitched in anticipation. "But the story can't end there," she wailed. "Did you find out if they died in the explosion? Did they, or any other members of the Book Club give chase?"

"Not that I know of. As you can imagine, I didn't want to stay around and wait to find out. I couldn't fly back to my crash site, with an AM reactor in my luggage; the humans would have discovered it and thought it was a weapon. Besides, the others might have been waiting for me at an airport. So I did the only other thing possible; I walked and hitchhiked there. It took me weeks. Somewhere in Sri Lanka, perhaps a few days or weeks after my final departure, the police might have discovered a dead white human male, washed up on one of he beaches, with most of his innards missing. It might have made front-page news, or maybe not.

"I could mention the Hydgol warship that passed me, four and a half years into my journey. I switched off all the power sources on my ship for hours and almost suffocated, hoping that I wouldn't be detected. It's not that I consider myself a fugitive or anything, but I didn't honestly know if the Hydgol would be pleased to see me or not. Well, if they did spot me, they didn't much care. That reactor held enough antimatter to make it this far. Now I'm taking a quick break and looking for other travel options." His tale dribbled to a halt. After his time spent on Earth, this seemed an appropriate time to shrug but, alas, this body had no shoulders. "And you know the rest." He concluded hastily.

Yakktranathac reached out a claw and turned off the recorder. I like it." She said, after a while, after ingesting some broth. "It may need a few details changed, particularly the dénouement and the way Earth culture's depicted. Might need to change a few names and things, but I think we have a promising storyline there."

"I look forward to reading it."

KRADDITHO

His skin was so cold; this I could tell without even getting anywhere close to touching it. In the muted light, I could already see the clammy sheen upon it and a pallid grey colour that told me of bloodlessness, or at least an absence of anything which I would recognise as blood. His shoulders appeared hunched but then his physiology was entirely unknown to me and perhaps they were meant to appear so. His face was permanently thrust forward by a colossal, elongated skull that constricted slightly at the base and then fused straight into his bony upper torso, producing an overall shape similar to the twin bulges within a peanut shell. His skull was ridged in many places by unfamiliar bone formations; he hadn't a single hair and no visible ears; his nose and lips appeared shrivelled and withdrawn, as if he had spent a year or so sunbathing without break in the middle of the Sahara and this exposed his immaculate rows of white teeth. Human teeth, as far as I could see. White teeth and white eyes, staring straight ahead, with undeniable intelligence from their sunken orbits. Eyes with dark brown irises that sparkled despite the shadow cast by the overhang of his enlarged brow. It was the eyes more than anything that made me suspect he had once been human. Perhaps not within his own lifetime but certainly of human ancestry. But who could say? I'm no expert.

His long, grey, bony fingers reached through the metal bars and tented themselves in a gesture that might have been construed as pleading for some but in this case seemed to speak only humility and calm contemplation of a grim situation.

"You don't know how long I've waited for another to come and speak with me," he said quietly. His accent was unplaceable and his lips struggled to produce the plosives of "come" and "speak", suggesting that perhaps English wasn't his language of choice but I had no difficulty in understanding him.

What you could not understand so easily was how I'd come to be standing here in the first place, face to face with this alarming creature. Less than five minutes earlier, I had been sitting down to drink at Max's Wine Bar, in a back road off of Chancery Lane and, after a slightly frustrating journey of twists and turns through narrow old, wood-panelled passageways looking for a place to relieve myself, I had clearly opened the wrong door and ended up in a place that totally defied my comprehension. It had to be some sort of prison complex; that much was evident from the barred, cell-like constructions that stretched down the huge, echoing corridor in both directions. However, the crumbling architecture bore no similarity to any I'd seen before, resembling a kind of once-shiny onyx, carved into strange-looking forms that you could only make out from the shine where distant light hit them. Were these forms abstract, or representations of creatures even stranger than the living one in the cage before me? That was something I preferred not to contemplate.

I could see no sign of movement in any of the other cells and the only sounds heard were that of the creature's wheezing breath and an occasional amorphous echo that could be a heavy door slamming in the extreme distance. There were one or two piles of debris dimly visible in different cells, which might have been discarded junk, damaged bits and pieces of the structure or simply things that had simply lived in them for too long. The light which I saw was faintly greenish in tint and was provided by snaking glass tubes in the ceiling, which looked as if they were circulating some luminescent chemical. An offensively musty smell, mixed perhaps with brick dust assailed my nostrils but I tolerated it for the moment, not least because it was probably masking far more unpleasant odours.

"Where exactly am I?" This had been one of the first questions I'd asked upon arriving here, naturally enough. Perhaps I'd said it with a more frightened tone to my voice the first time around, which could explain why the thing didn't comprehend and had instead babbled about eternal silences and misery, or some-such. The question had come after my initial shocked reaction when I saw the thing that had called out to you from behind its bars - a reaction that I had then dutifully apologised for.

"Here? Where is here? Sometimes I wonder if the question means anything any more. I think I knew other places once but how do I know now that I'd not imagined them? You're the first proof I've seen in aeons that this alone is not the universe."

"Mate, this is the basement of a wine bar near Holborn Tube Station."

He – I stopped for the first time to ask myself if it was really a he, as the voice was almost androgynous and, due to the poor lighting and its forward stoop, I could not make out its lower body in detail. This was probably a blessing. Something about its face had seemed to be masculine. Anyway – he looked back at me with an expression of total bafflement, brow folding itself into a surprised arch of rubbery flesh. "I don't know anything of Tube Stations. My name is Kradditho and I was twelfth Grand Astrologer to Corrusbowth XXIV, back in the Fifth Echelon of Belshazaar." He paused expectantly, looking at me in the hope that this might mean something important to me but now it was evidently my turn to look confused.

"I'm Colin," I managed.

The creature extended its hand and I shook it, trying not to wince when I felt it to be even colder than I'd expected. The bony object withdrew once more into the cell.

"Look, umm, are there prison guards around here or anything? I don't mean to be, like, rude but would I get in trouble if someone catches me here?"

Kradditho looked from side to side, surveying the empty corridor. "No, they very rarely come down here. Maybe once a week, to feed me." My gaze fell upon a metal tray, half-pushed underneath the cage door. A couple of stained, misshapen-looking bones lay upon it. "They are slow and stupid, you could easily leave before they harm you."

"Ri-i-i-ght." Up until that point I'd half-hoped that there was a more innocent explanation for this place but that evidently wasn't the case. "So… who exactly are *they?*"

"My tormentors – I fear their true name would be unpronounceable to you. They were such vile masters to me; millennia ago I tried to trick them and they imprisoned me here as punishment. You see these pits on the inside of my cell?"

Sure enough, in the areas of floor not masked by shadow, I could see thousands of tiny indentations in the surface, perhaps twenty-five or thirty to a square inch. These indentations seemed to carry on up the inward-facing sides of the bars and, presumably, up the interior walls as well. You shivered with the realisation that each of these must represent a day of his confinement.

"Don't ask me now how many. I ran out of space long, long ago. They are a terrible, cruel hearted race of monsters."

Did he mean monsters in a metaphorical way? I decided not to ask.

"That's, umm, *really* bad."

Kradditho nodded, by bending his entire body.

The words sounded worse than stupid before they'd even left my mouth but I couldn't bear the silence. "Like, really bad."

"Yes."

Another awkward pause.

"But how exactly did I get here? I mean, this can't be London, right?"

A tear began to well in Kradditho's eye. "I don't know where this is any more."

"Oh. Come on, don't cry." I searched my pockets for a clean tissue but didn't seem to have one. Kradditho turned away into the shadows, as if to conceal his emotions from me.

“Look mate, is there anything I can do? You know, is there a way out for you?”

Turning back to face me, he looked as if he was about to say something but then sadly shook his head.

I’d told Lauren that I was working late. This tends to be an excuse used about six or seven times each month when I didn’t feel like going home straight away and felt like being alone instead. Just one or two drinks, followed by a quick gargle of Listerine to remove the smell before I get on the train home. We’ve been married for four years now and sometimes I just feel that personal space is becoming a bit too much of a rare thing sometimes. Especially since Serena was born as well; the house became, naturally enough, a noisier and smaller place. For some time it bothered me that I ought to be a more attentive husband at such a time but I’m really only missing out on a handful of hours a month, so I don’t see that it’s a big deal. The temptation is to do this more often but then maybe it would be harmful, so I don’t. Serena’s getting closer to that age when she starts to quieten down a little bit and, before too long, she’ll be starting school. She seems to have shot up so quickly already that I wouldn’t be surprised if she starts tomorrow; she comes in to lie down with me and Lauren less frequently now during the nights and she cries less. At this rate I might even have a sex life back eventually.

Drinking alone bothers some people; they seem to associate it with losers and alcoholics but I think it can be relaxing in its own kind of way. A meditative, spiritualising activity, taking ever slower lung-fulls of that unique pub air and gazing dreamily into space beneath the blinking lights of a fruit machine, moving only occasionally to take another sip of whiskey or to swirl the diminishing ice cubes around in the bottom of the glass, watching the prismatic effect of light passing through them and listening to jukebox music or football commentary and ambient bullshit conversations that drift intertwined with the smoke.

Usually my watering hole of choice for this was The Goat And Bell but on this particular night I walked in, noticed some familiar colleagues clustered in one corner and didn't fancy getting into work-related conversations, so I walked back out, hopefully before they noticed me. I needed a quick substitute place and Max's had been the first that presented itself. Only a couple of other customers, who had looked like regulars, probably fused to their bar stools by the process of fossilisation. The barman had regarded me wearily through the drifting haze and served a Scotch in a slightly grimy-looking tumbler; then I had taken up a seat of my own, semi-consciously mimicking the postures of the other wasters here, slowly turning the glass around in my hand and tapping it gently against the formica counter, as if I was perhaps conducting a subtle forensic test on the various particles which crusted its surfaces. I contemplated money issues and fixing the car for a bit, while the compass needle in my brain turned at a leisurely pace, until it could settle upon a definite topic of thought. I waited for a while until nature began to take its course and then I got up and wandered aimlessly between unmarked doors and creaking downward staircase, searching for the bogs.

* * * *

"This is my wife and my daughter," I explained, pointing at the small, creased photo in my wallet. Kradditho's eyes became animated, seeming to scan every last detail of the image. Rosaline was born of a white father and black mother; her features were mainly caucasian but with dark eyes and a frizz to her hair that she spent a lot of time and effort making features out of. The two of us had met at a previous job, drawn together initially by a mutual taste for science fiction movies and the occasional late night trip to the seclusion of a park during summer. I had dated for just a few months before getting engaged and we'd seemed to rumble ever faster down the subway line of commitment, with the attendant stations blurring always more rapidly past the windows until I began to wonder where on earth I was and how I'd got there. I'd sometimes wondered whether or not my parents harboured any objections to mixed-race relationships - they'd never come across as being like that during my childhood but I was never a hundred percent sure if they'd make a wrong move when confronted with a situation like this. But they seemed fine with it in the end, as supportive as I could have wished and helped us out loads with the marriage.

Serena came along during the third year of the relationship and I'd been pretty pleased with how she came out. A lot of my old friends were dads by that time and I suppose I always did have a bit of a problem with feeling left behind, although even after hearing their stories of child-rearing, I don't think either of us had been fully prepared for the hard work we'd let ourselves in for. Lauren picked herself up from it somewhat more easily than I had though; recently she'd been talking about having a second brat and this time it caused a bit of friction as I don't think I'm up to it. This is surely one of the reasons why I now take these short sanity breaks after work some days before the long journey home. Well, 'sanity breaks' until a short while ago. It had become difficult, standing in a prison in another time/dimension/universe/planet when all I'd expected to find was a urinal, a couple of stalls and a condom machine that doesn't work. I think I dealt with it all pretty well, to be honest.

I wondered how much of my family life Kradditho understood from looking at the picture. Did they even have photographs or portraits where he came from? He didn't seem fazed by the sight of the printed scrap. I'd not known whether showing him pictures was a really great idea - it might do him good to see glimpses of the outside world, even if it's obviously not *his* world. On the other hand, it might have upset him more if he had a family of his own somewhere, so I'd hesitated. In the end he begged to see whatever things I could show him, so he got the guided tour of my wallet contents and a few snapshot saved on my phone. For him it must have been like a weekend trip to Las Vegas. Or Blackpool, anyway.

Kradditho also became excited when he caught sight of my pocket week-to-view diary. I flicked through the pages to demonstrate to him that it was just full of handwritten notes, probably of no interest to him but his eyes became glassy just at the notion of seeing a book again.

"You, uh, you have books where you're from then?"

Kradditho vanished into the shadowy depths of his cell and returned with a filthy, vaguely rectangular object which he offered me through the bars. I immediately regretted taking it, as the heavy thing, bound in what had presumably once been leather, looked like it was centuries old. It was encrusted with some moist black substance, similar to peat and when I gingerly prised it open the pages that remained were covered more thickly with mould than any printed characters.

"This is the last one they gave me," he explained as I tried my best not to look disgusted with the object. "Do you know how many times I've read it?"

"No, how many times?"

He paused and a vacant look crept across his face. "I'm actually not sure."

The text was certainly not in any language or alphabet that you recognised. Each page seemed to be divided neatly into a grid, with squiggly-looking black glyphs bordered within each square. I had no idea which direction to read them in, or if indeed I was actually holding the tome the right way up.

"D'you think I could, um, *have this*? There are people I know who'd find it really interesting." This was a lie; I didn't know any language professors or anybody like that. But I could surely find one if I tried hard enough and I'm sure they'd pay a lot of money to get their hands on this book, filthy or not.

"No!" Kradditho wailed, with an abrupt change in tone that startled me. "I could never bear to part with it!"

After causing a couple of its more decayed pages to fall out with my inexpert handling, I decided to hurriedly pass it back. For a fleeting moment I thought something had been left behind on my hand; it looked kind of like an uncurling, grey caterpillar and I tried to swipe it off in panic but the thing was suddenly no longer there; must either have been a sliver of rotten paper or my imagination.

"How come you can speak English anyway?"

Kradditho lovingly returned the book to the recesses of his cell and then returned to face me, seeming more composed. "I can make myself understood to anybody as I see fit. It is one of my many talents."

This threw me. TV had long ago introduced me to the notion of Universal Translators but I didn't see him using any kind of electronic device, or even a wriggling fish for that matter. His lips seemed to be moving in sync with his speech, so perhaps he was able to pluck language directly out of my head? Or – a possibility which had been more than slightly lurking in my conscience – I had gone insane. My drink might have been spiked or I might have hit my head on something while I was searching for the toilets. Maybe this is what schizophrenia is like? Was I lying at the bottom of those creaking stairs in a wine bar basement, waiting to be discovered by the surly-looking barman? This wasn't a practical joke anyway; I'd sussed that much right from the beginning. This was no set and Kradditho was no puppet or actor in makeup.

“Do any other people like me come down here to visit you?”

Kradditho looked confused. “I don’t believe so. How I'd like to get out of here and meet more people."

I nodded and turned my attention back to the cell itself. "What are these bars actually made of?" On closer examination, they didn't seem that much like metal but a rough and almost stone-like texture. There appeared to be no lock or bolts for what I'd taken to be a door: what kept it closed was a mystery, unless the thing had actually been modified to make it unopenable.

“Oh. Look, I’m still a bit freaked out about how I got here in the first place. If you don’t know either, then I think I should go back and try to figure out if that door to the toilets is still there—“

There was another sob from within the cell. “Please don’t leave me. If you go, at least promise you’ll come back. Can you even imagine what it’s like to be confined here for more years than you can possibly count?”

“No, but—“

“And if nothing is done then my suffering might go on until the end of time itself!”

I was beginning to feel a bit of unease mix with my pity at this point. He was right though; obviously I couldn’t imagine the position he was in. “Mate, I don’t even know what happened that made me get here. I thought I was at least meant to walk through a wardrobe or something, not… ever mind. Look, if I can help you, I will okay?” I turned and began to walk at that point, not actually having any idea whether I could help him or not. There came a torrent of pleading and blubbering from behind me, which was barely comprehensible. Sure, I felt sorry for the poor bastard but what was I supposed to do? I came out for a quiet drink not to get tangled up in jail breaks or whatever he was trying to hint at. I was out of my depth and really needed to come up for air.

"Same again?" Asked the bartender, oblivious to the paleness of my face when I sat down again on the high stool. He probably assumed I'd gone downstairs to have a puke or something.

"Uhh, no. Can I have a coffee instead?"

"Don't do coffee, pal."

"Anything with… oh sod it, okay same again, then. Make it a double this time."

Another Scotch was pushed in front of me and I downed it in a gulp. I paid and made one more trip downstairs as a last check to see if I was sane or not. Found the correct door to the gents toilets; there are gents toilets on the other side. Returned to the unmarked door I'd previously tried (it looked, on a second inspection, more like a broom cupboard or storage room): a faintly chilly breeze hit me and there was huge and otherworldly prison corridor. Kradditho perhaps saw the light from the door opening in the distance and began to call out faintly to me, waving his arms. For the first time, it occurred to me to use my camera phone as proof, so I took the device out of my pocket and ran off a couple of snaps before backing out of the door and plodding upstairs again. The space was too big and dark – the shots I'd taken simply looked black when I viewed them on the little screen. Fucksticks. I'd been about to show them to the barman and ask him if he recognised the place but instead I simply returned the phone to my pocket and strolled out into the cold drizzle and failing daylight of bustling London.

I re-immersed myself in home life that evening, seeing that my usual complexion had at last returned and my brain was obviously filing the earlier events in the "You're probably best off not going there" drawer and preparing to lose the key. Kradditho's stinking, monochrome world gave way to the peach-scented conditioner in Lauren's hair as she embraced me; bulbous, brightly coloured plastic children's toys; evening television; food, coffee, a plane crash in Italy, Serena's excited babblings as she looked at pictures of animals in a book; bed sheets and darkness. We tried to initiate sex but she was tired and so was I and the whole thing ran unceremoniously out of energy during the foreplay.

Work the next day was the same; the usual fluorescent-lit human zoo to which I'd been accustomed for some time, shackled to my keyboard and occasionally watching the clouds roll by through the window or joining in banter with colleagues about *Eastenders* or football. I left at five and this time carefully avoided any place for a drinking stop-over – especially Max's of course - picking up Serena from the day-care centre, arriving home before Lauren for once and telling her that the office had shut early because of electrical problems. The only intrusion of the surreal into this day had been playing with my phone while I rode on the train and noticing the two ominous, black photos still saved in the memory. Somehow I felt it would be wrong to delete them and instead I found myself skipping past them to look at other images instead, like my mother's dog or my mates and their girlfriends. There was a small line visible on one of my hands – I assumed this to be a paper cut from handling that weird book yesterday, although it seemed odd that something so damp, moldy and worn could still have sharp edges. The train rattled onwards towards home and my mind turned to other things.

My first dream about Kradditho was that night. It stuck out far clearer in my memory than most dreams, probably because of its extremely vivid imagery. Kradditho being led out into a stone courtyard strung with banners by human soldiers, everybody – including, ludicrously, the prisoner - dressed in French Revolution-period clothing. He was dragged to the top of a scaffold and I watched him bending down into a guillotine and the blade plummeting down into his thick, immovable, pseudo-neck and saw the arcing sprays of unfamiliar bodily fluids from his many severed tubes. His wizened body convulsed and the big, grey, peanut-shaped head dropped with a bony thud into the basket. I was standing in the crowd; a crowd which had jeered at him and erupted in thunderous jubilation at his death. I suppose my subconscious mind is not a very subtle dramatist when it wants to make a point; he hadn't ever mentioned awaiting execution but the principle remained.

The dreams recurred over a series of a few nights, causing me to toss and turn sometimes violently in bed. While the exact scenario of Kradditho's death changed each night, the underlying idea remained all too obviously the same. One night he was left behind on a crashing plane by the rest of the crew who all had parachutes; another time he was messily torn to pieces by lions on the floor of a Roman arena. When it was not the dreams it was insomnia and I would lie for what seemed like hours, string upwards and trying to make out details of the bedroom ceiling in the gloom – the paper lampshade, the rose, the bumps in the plaster – until I would eventually succumb to dream-space again just before dawn. Lauren mentioned a couple of occasions where I mumbled in my sleep. To my relief, she apparently couldn't discern any particular words or phrases, although it must have been all too obvious to her that something was distressing me and I began to feel awkward making excuses for this night time behaviour. Serena noticed it as well, for she stopped visiting us during the night altogether.

I passed Max's wine bar one Friday, as I was taking a stroll during my lunch break. Taking a sideways peek through the windows as I passed, I recognised the same barman I'd seen before and a handful of my office worker brethren, sitting around nibbling plates of chips and sandwiches. I thought again of the featureless, black photos that remained stored on my phone's memory card. Something occurred to me – not for the first time, although this time it seemed a little more relevant: what if I'd somehow had a temporary 'episode' that night? What if it were possible for me to go totally doolally for a period of just a few minutes without any warning and then return to normal again just as suddenly? And, if that were the case, where exactly had I been standing when I took those photographs? My best guess was that it was a dark cupboard or boiler room. If I proved this theory to myself right here and now, it seemed like a surefire route back to sleeping normally. One-off temporary madness was not a pleasant thing to know I've been through, but at least if I knew that was all it was, then I could just put it behind me and never need tell anybody.

I strolled into the place and headed for the stairs down, expecting the barman to stop me and say the toilets were for paying customers only. He didn't even look up from his newspaper and I continued on my way. I found the corridor to the toilets empty as before and paused in front of the unmarked door to the netherworld. I took a deep breath. I really hoped I was only going to discover something ordinary and mundane on the other side. Shutting my eyes, I pushed it open.

"Colin! Colin! Oh my saviour, you have returned to liberate me!"

Keeping my eyes tightly closed, I backed out again and let the door close itself. Great. It was one thing to pass beggars in the street without giving them any money; I always felt sympathy for people with no homes and whatever, but you can't walk down street in some areas without seeing at least one. God only knows how many people are homeless in London alone and if I did everything I could to help them I wouldn't even make a dent in the problem. So, like most other commuters, I'd learned long ago to turn my head and carry on with my journey. Could I treat Kradditho in the same way? This moral dilemma wasn't going to stop haunting me and he was just one individual and not a horde, so I suppose I was trapped. There was only one course of action and I left the bar again, hurriedly walking the streets with a worried expression, hunting for the nearest shop selling tools. I muttered to myself again and again as I examined glass display cabinets full of drills and angle grinders, how insane this was and how I couldn't believe I was doing it. A further worry, which quickly dawned upon me as I entered the first DIY store and spoke to the sales assistant, was that I didn't actually know what the bars of the cell were made from, so I was forced to make a few half-hearted statements about needing cutting tools 'just for general purpose cutting of things, you know.'

I just wanted to be free of the obligation I felt I'd stumbled into and using up a bit of emergency cash on tools seemed, right then and there, like a reasonable price to pay in order to put the whole episode behind me and resume living my life - besides, I could always sell them to somebody after they'd served their purpose. Time was ticking until my manager expected me back in the office and I plumped for a pair of long-handled bolt cutters, a large hammer, a hacksaw and a small blowtorch, powered by a disposable gas canister. It also occurred to me that, no matter how dosey he might be, the bartender might object to me walking down to the toilets with armfuls of destructive-looking implements, so I also purchased a big, canvas tool bag to carry them in.

Returning to the winding, wood-panelled passage beneath Max's Wine Bar, I crossed over once again into whatever plane of space and time I'd been exploring and headed for the still-pleading creature in the corridor of otherwise empty cells.

"I knew you'd return! Praise be to Colin, the greatest man of any age!"

I wasn't in the mood for long speeches, so with only a cursory greeting, I dropped the bag to the floor, unzipped it and gestured to Kradditho stand back as I began attacking the bars with the hacksaw. It was hard work and the blade made a protesting sound but some fine, glittery powder began to collect on the floor at my feet and after a minute or so I noticed that the blade had made a small amount of progress. It would take perhaps an hour to remove two bars and my boss wouldn't like me being away from my desk for that long - I'd need to have been in a road accident or something to pull that one off. Perhaps mildly more threatening was the prospect of one of these hitherto-unseen jailers turning up and catching me in the act. No, I really didn't want to get sucked any deeper into this nightmare, so something faster was needed. Using a cigarette lighter, I fired up the blowtorch and started working on softening the bars. Using a combination of saw blade and bolt cutter on the glowing metal, within about ten minutes I had removed a section about four feet in length. I still had no idea what it was made of but it was damned heavy and it made a booming clang when I laid it down on the floor, which didn't seem to bring any guards running but certainly didn't make me feel any more comfortable. Kradditho began to get very excited at this point, placing his face dangerously close to where I was working and babbling so quickly that I could no longer tell if he was speaking English or some completely unknown language. I had managed to get an oil stain on my work shirt. Great - the 'I got run over' excuse was starting to sound more and more appealing as the minutes ticked by. One of my few comforts was that I seemed to have no phone reception here, wherever here was, so no calls from the office checking up on my whereabouts.

As I began to saw through the second bar I felt a faint but detectable vibration pulsing through its fabric. This unnerved me a bit, especially since Kradditho was unable to explain exactly what was causing it. The bar, like all of its counterparts, disappeared into the ceiling and made me feel that perhaps it was connected to something beyond. I couldn't leave the job half-finished of course; Kradditho couldn't possibly escape through the hole I'd created so far and he'd most likely be in serious trouble if a guard found what I'd done. I was a hundred percent committed now, so I continued to saw with renewed vigour, uttering a silent prayer to a god I had long since stopped believing in, that the saw blade wouldn't give out on me and need replacing.

I took the loose section of bar in both hands and, bracing myself against its weight, lifted it down and placed it on the floor. As I slid it out from the place it had occupied for aeons, the cell itself began to emit a frightening, high-pitched scream, as if every surface was alive and vibrating in unison. The sound seemed to bore through my skull with its intensity and my immediate reaction was that it must be an alarm of some sort. Kradditho seemed less concerned about it and, with a child-like excitement that I'd never before witnessed in his behaviour, squeezed his body through the gap and out into the corridor, where he stood, trembling, gazing up and down the corridor of empty cells and back into his own, now vacant space, spellbound by the fact that he was now seeing it from an unfamiliar perspective. I paused in my activity, noticing that I could see his entire figure clearly for the first time. His head/body seemed to taper towards the abdomen and terminated in a short, pointed tail that probably no longer served any purpose. His two spindly legs, while being grey and hairless like the rest of him, were like those of a goat, with knees that bent the opposite way to a human's and ending in feet that were small and hoof-like. My assumption that he was male appeared to be correct, as a narrow, flaccid penis hung between his legs. It had a ridged appearance, making it appear almost like an overgrown earthworm. No visible testicles. Interesting - had he been castrated at some point in the past, or perhaps they were integrated with his abdomen in some way?

The sound did not stop and while Kradditho turned around and around on the spot, marveling at the decaying surroundings, I was throwing the tools back into the bag and preparing to make a sharp exit. As I straightened up and hoisted the clanking collection of things onto my shoulder, I noticed something in the distance that had not been there a few moments earlier. I couldn't tell exactly what it was, but it appeared to be big and heading towards us.

"Shit! I've got to go. It was nice meeting you and everything but I've got a life to get back to."

I began to hurry in the direction of my own world but I heard Kradditho's footsteps clicking after me. The wailing alarm-sound began at last to fade and die, although in its place I could now hear an urgent skittering of the newcomer as it rushed closer to us. I also thought I heard an indignant squealing sound, the sort of sound a wild animal might make when cornered. I couldn't find the courage to turn and look at whatever it was.

"You can't come with me!"

"But I have to!" Kradditho wailed. "Where else can I go?"

"I-- well, I don't know! I thought you knew how to get back to your own place. Didn't you think about that before you asked me to bust you out?"

"*Anywhere* is better than here! Do you not realise what will happen if that beast catches me now?"

We'd almost reached the door. On both sides, the door was made from faded and chipped pine-panelling, with a small brass handle. In my world it was the kind of door you wouldn't look twice at but it looked distinctly out of place in the intricately carved, onyx wall of an inhuman prison corridor. I thought I could faintly detect sounds of a pub on the other side of it. There were a million riddles tied to the presence of this door here but I knew I'd never know the answers to them; besides, there were more pressing issues at hand. What if the prison guard could follow me through it, for one thing? Placing my hand on the handle to open it, I finally turned around to see how close our pursuer was. It was moving at about human jogging-pace (not really that slow, then) and would reach us in a few more seconds. I had previously found myself wondering why the corridor had such high ceilings and if this creature was its principal user, then that would explain things. It must have been at least nine feet tall and totally inhuman in shape. It had a podular, bloated body, from which extended dozens of appendages for performing a variety of tasks. It was moving towards us on a collection of long, thin, flexing tentacles that were making the awful skittering sound as they brushed on the smooth floor and lifting its main body well clear of the ground. This gave it the look of a floating balloon, trailing ropes and cords beneath it. Other limbs didn't seem to have a use at this particular moment, although I really didn't want to find out what they did when it caught up with me. A cluster of orifices, short, waving feelers and snout-like growths at the front of its body was presumably what passed as a face. I'd considered threatening it with the hammer but this now seemed like a suicidally bad idea.

"Ple-e-ease!" Kradditho trilled.

"Look, I don't think my world is really your..."

I looked again at the monster pursuing us.

"Okay, come on, quick!"

We both rushed through the doorway and I slammed it shut. There was nobody in the small passageway but the pub sounds and the drifting nicotine smell from upstairs indicated that I was surely back on my own turf. Kradditho continued to look around, eyes wide, taking it all in. I couldn't hear the screeching or skittering of the prison guard any more. Just perfectly ordinary pub toilet ambience, although I still kept my distance from that door, worried that a tentacle might come through it and try to grab me.

"Right," I said breathlessly, then stalled as I tried to follow it up with something meaningful. "Right, we've been through a lot together and everything, but this is like, my city, you know? Full of people like me. You're not gonna fit in. You'll get taken away and dissected or something."

He seemed totally unbothered by this. "It's beautiful," he said in hushed reverence for the yellowed pine panelling, dirty carpet and tatty wall-lamps with flickering orange candle-effect bulbs. "I will like it here."

"Yeah. Well, like I say, I'm not really sure how you're gonna get by in London. You might be better off looking for another door leading somewhere else, you know? If it happened here, then perhaps you can go to other places too. Me; I've got a wife and a kid, I can't go 'round with creatures from... uh.."

"The Fifth Echelon of Belshazaar."

"Right. Yeah. Well, glad we understand each other, an' all." I moved to shake his hand but he didn't seem familiar with the gesture and continued to look at me with innocent and expectant eyes. I began to walk away from him, already thinking about heading home to change my shirt and what excuse I could make to my manager but he still wouldn't shut up.

"This is some kind of establishment for alcohol, is that right?"

"Uhh, yeah, it is. I've got to--"

"Then I say we should both celebrate my escape with a beverage. Is that customary in your culture?"

I was no longer trying to hide the discomfort in my expression. "No, I don't think that's a good idea."

"Why?"

I was getting angry now. "Did you listen to anything I just said?"

"Oh, you're worried about my appearance? Your people have such simple perceptions of form. I can make them see whatever I want them to - they won't be the least bit disturbed." He brushed past me and led the way up the stairs to the bar, beckoning me to follow. I did so, but keeping the most discrete distance I could and then paused on the half-landing, waiting for the first horrified shrieks of other customers when they saw him. But there were none.

I rounded the corner to discover Kradditho seated precariously on top of one of the tall bar stools, studying a copy of the wine list. The barman stood nearby, regarding the new customer with his usual look of professional disinterest. I hovered uncertainly near to Kradditho for a few moments, gripped by a perverse fascination with this situation. Did he really have some sort of manipulative mind control over other beings? Small pockets of office workers still sat around the place, downing glasses of wine or beer whilst keeping a careful eye on their watches. They showed no interest in the alien being in their midst.

"Good thing you're here," he said when he looked up and noticed me. "Here, take a seat. I took the liberty of ordering you Chilean cabernet sauvignon; I understand from this fellow that it's a particularly good example of wine."

"No, thanks, I have to be going." I continued edging towards the door. Kradditho and also the barman watched me, causing me to feel increasingly uneasy.

"Colin," he continued, his voice now lowered somewhat in tone. "I don't have any currency with which to pay for this drinking. I told the proprietor here that you would be so good as to pay for it."

"What?" I gasped, dismayed.

The barman continued to stare at me, looking ever less pleased.

"Please don't embarrass us both," Kradditho pleaded through clenched teeth.

I let out a weary sigh and moved back to the bar and pulled up a stool.

"That's nine-fifty," said the barman and I irritably slapped a note down on the counter. He held it up to the light and examined it with the expression of somebody who was concerned I might have used it for toilet paper.

"Look, you can't behave like this," I said to Kradditho in a hushed voice. "I know you're a stranger here and you don't know our customs, but..." My voice trailed off as I noticed something disturbing on the floor by the base of Kradditho's stool. There were two - no, three small, squirming grey things like overgrown maggots, waving their front ends about to blindly taste the air before undulating their ways in different directions over the dirty carpet. There was a quiet plop as a fourth dropped from Kradditho's seat and joined them. My expression froze in absolute horror as I noticed a couple more emerging from small, hitherto unnoticed orifices in the sides of his bare torso. I made a sound that probably sounded a bit like "Wub?"

Kradditho winked at me. "Don't mind them. Not the prettiest of things but entirely necessary, I assure you." It occurred to me for the first time that these things resembled the thing I had brushed from my arm a few days earlier, when I first visited the other world. Evidently it wasn't a scrap of moldy paper then. And there was still a faintly visible blemish on my skin there - I shuddered at the thought that it might have bitten me. I made a very passionate mental note to visit the doctor as soon as I could to get myself checked out.

He dismissed the matter with a camp wave of his hand. "As you so rightly pointed out just now, Colin, I am not a creature of this world and there is a lot of which I have no understanding. You understand, of course, that without you I'd be completely alone."

"You seem to be doing alright so far," I hissed, looking at the generous wine glass in front of him.

"But what is this?" He continued. "This is not a life, this is just a moment, pleasant though it is. No, I have a lot of work lying ahead if I am to take root and flourish. I need knowledge to do this."

"Then go to a library. You've got what you wanted from me and I don't remember even asking for anything in return." I pushed my own glass away across the counter, as if to underscore the point. Without noticing, I'd spilt some of it when I'd recoiled in alarm from Kradditho's maggots (which now seemed to have crawled away and vanished from sight).

"No," he mused, seemingly totally impervious to my anger. "You're quite right, you've not asked me for any reward, even though it would have been perfectly understandable for you to do so."

"Yeah. Well." I wished I could have found better parting words, or words that had actually meant something for that matter, but his attitude was really bothering me by this stage and I wanted to cut myself free of it while I still had the chance. I stood and picked up my bag, quickly inspecting it in case one of those grubs had crawled onto it.

"A man like yourself could go so far in such a simple world," he said, now with what might have been a wry smile. "You've no idea what I could do for you."

"Yeah. Well, whatever." I turned my back on him and walked to the door. As I approached it, I was propelled backwards by a sudden flash of heat and concussive shock. I landed painfully on my arse and looking up, saw that that a punter sitting by the door had just been decapitated and a pall of greasy looking smoke was now rising from where his head had been and fanning outwards when it reached the ceiling tiles. I felt wetness on my face and looked down to see that I was spattered with blood and bone fragments. So was the wall next to where the man had sat and also the face and blouse of the woman he'd been drinking with. She didn't actually seem to have noticed though and went on casually puffing her fag, an attitude echoed by all the other lunchtime drinkers, who only seemed interested in the fact that I'd just fallen over. After a few seconds of deliberating, his torso flopped sideways out of the seat and thudded onto the carpet where it continued to smoulder and ooze. The smell was hideous.

I turned back to face Kradditho, who still perched upon his stool and was theatrically pointing a forefinger towards the seat where the man had been sitting. Presumably this gesture was performed just for my benefit, as he lowered it once he saw that I'd noticed it.

"Now, I feel I ought to appologise for that," he smiled pleasantly.

"However, the way you behaved just now was thoroughly rude and I didn't like the tone of it. Would you return to your seat and let's continue with our conversation, shall we?"

I picked myself up and returned to my stool.

"I want to make it clear to you that I don't need your help specifically. I could ask these favours of any person you see around us. But that would be a pity Colin, really it would. You've demonstrated to me through your actions what a bright and - above all - conscientious person you are. I *like* you and I value your friendship, so it really would be sad for you to let me down and make me choose another. Are you hungry?"

I nodded weakly. My vision momentarily lighted on Kradditho's odd, scrotumless cock, which lay before him on the vinyl stool cover.

"What are... pork *scratchings?* What are those?" he asked.

"They're sort of like bits of fat, or something. Sometimes with hair, I think."

"I say we share a bag full of those, what do you say? Or should we have a bag each?"

I waved to the bartender and paid for two packets. As he turned to retrieve them from the shelving behind the bar, I noticed one of the grey grub-creatures concertina-ing its way up the front of his shirt. He seemed oblivious to it.

"Good. Now, there are a few basic things I will need to establish before I get started proper. Tell me about the political systems that are used to govern this world."

"There's, umm, lots of different countries and..." The bartender returned with the greasy snacks and I noticed the squirming creature now clinging to his neck, still aparently without his knowledge. Before my eyes, it wriggled and seemed to bury its front end into the man's soft tissue and disappeared with a flourish, leaving behind only a very small hole which closed without any blood. I paid him for the scratchings and he returned to polishing some glasses with a filthy rag.

"Tell me about this country first," Kradditho said, his patient tone reminding me now of a primary school teacher.

"We're a democracy and we... have a a queen as well but we don't elect her and she doesn't really do very much, but we have political parties and... and..."

The woman sitting opposite the decapitated man had now removed a small mirror from her handbag and was calmly applying lipstick while another of the small creatures wriggled into her neck and vanished.

The mass public-transportation system of my life continued to rumble along its divine tracks while I watched the blur of passing events from over the top of my newspaper. Occasionally a particular image that I noticed would stick in my mind, like perhaps an arguing couple glimpsed as a platform drifted by or a stroboscopic freezeframe of passengers on board another train, as it rushed by in the opposite direction. The four of us were happy living together; I remember being so pleased with the acceptance and warm affection with which Lauren and Serena welcomed the new family member and how pleased we all were with the practical advice with which he soon began to enhance our lives. New skills meant that both Lauren and I were soon out of our nine-to-fives and climbing the entreprenurial ladder of opportunity, while our daughter excelled so much at school that she was soon moved ahead two years and then on to private, specialist education, which we were by that time easily able to afford.

Kradditho, as I'd suspected right from the start, has gone into politics and he's doing amazingly well, bringing me up to date each morning on his latest plans and their progress.

I remember also, the evening that I told Serena that she was going to have a new brother or sister. I'd not been at all worried, explaining that the fifth family member was going to be her half-sister and not my own flesh and blood. Maybe he or she wouldn't look quite like her but I know that they'd both get on and no-one would need to feel excluded. After all, she's a bright girl and I knew she'd understand the importance of it and that she would still remain special in our eyes as well, even if not in quite the same way. Lauren is very excited too - we'll be able to take on absolutely anything then, the five of us.

It can be a long and occasionally very bumpy journey but I suppose the only important thing is to have a map of all the stops you must call at - something which, until I met him, I'd lacked. When you can see exactly what's planned out ahead of you, the ride can be so fulfilling and purposeful.

NIGHT

Pausing to take some weight off my aching feet, I halted at the side of the narrow road and brushed some snow from the top of a rusty old metal drum, which made an acceptable seat. I drank some purified water from the flask in my webbing, tilted back my head and took in some deep breaths from the still air, letting it chill the inside of my chest and blowing it out again in a long spout of vapour. There was no sound around me, besides a gentle but frigid breeze. It was early July and the dense covering of cloud, acting together with the covering of snow, had so far reflected away so much of the sun's heat that polar ice sheets had encroached as far south as Scotland and as far north as Patagonia, draining the oceans and creating yet more new land to become dressed in white.

That was my job; I, like hundreds of thousands of others across the world, painted things white. In some places the snow and ice simply couldn't find a foothold and I gave it a helping hand, using my battered tin of enamel and my threadbare brush which forever swung at my side.

The sun made a brief and rare appearance through a gap in the clouds and I fumbled for my scratched old goggles before the landscape around me lit up like one giant golden halo, threatening to burn my retinas. The sun was low in the sky – considerably lower in fact than I'd expected. Damn, that'd teach me to pay attention to the passage of time. It would set in barely more than an hour and I was still – I dismounted from the oil drum and checked my map – six miles out of the nearest town. That was bad. I'd have to seal up the paint can and run some of the way back there. I was still a young man, of course. I didn't carry as many memories of the world before the freeze and consequently my adjustment to the great changes had not been as difficult as it had been for some others around me.

Uncompacted virgin snow scrunched beneath my boots and I made my way hurriedly through a jungle of dead, brittle hedgerows, skeletal trees, half-submerged signposts and humps of abandoned vehicles; all the time trying to peer into the distance for any rising smoke that could indicate a settlement. Some way up ahead, the narrow country road joined a larger highway, one that was still kept clear and salted for motor vehicles to pass (although I had not heard the sound of an engine since yesterday).

Late evening descended, disguised as shadowless, diffuse light. The dead did not, for the most part, emerge during daylight hours - unless they were particularly hungry, but even then the harsh white glare overloaded their filmy, shrivelled eyes and rendered them confused and largely helpless. Night, on the other hand, was a different kettle of fish. These creatures, though technically still mammalian, operated something like reptiles now and though their metabolisms slowed the colder it got, the icy conditions which froze their limbs and made them brittle also slowed decay which might otherwise have eradicated them within a couple of weeks.

The sky was beginning to bruise when I stopped again. The clearway was only a few minutes further ahead but there was still no sound of any traffic that might give me a ride, just my own footsteps and harsh breathing. My bladder was almost full but I couldn't see anywhere practical to go without melting an obvious hole in the white. My thigh was sore from the constant slap-slap-slap of the paint can and my feet hurt worse than ever. I reminded myself that these concerns were trivial by comparison to what would happen if a dead person found me but what finally brought me to a stop was the sight of a conspicuously dark object suspended in the air. Very few of the old, overhead telephone cables were used nowadays and these ones were sagging dejectedly between their poles, yet they still supported the tangled mass of somebody's rucksack. It must have contained something, since it only swayed a little in the wind and it didn't appear to have been there long, judging from the light dusting of snow. A week at the very most…

A car-shaped mound was almost directly beneath the bag and the uneven distribution of snow on its roof and bonnet indicated where somebody had climbed up to purposely hang the bag there. Why? I decided that I could both satisfy my curiosity and use the vantage point to scan for any vehicles or other travellers, so I clambered onto the roof of the half-buried car and had a scan around the flat country surrounding me. There was the dark strip of black ice which was the highway but not a single thing moving. A solitary bird flapped in the distance – I'd read about birds as a child and been told that they were once common here – but otherwise the landscape was lifeless. Further away still, I could make out a solitary church spire and some pale grey rectangles that might have been part of a cityscape. Turning my attention the bag, I reached out and snagged it with my fingertips, brought it closer and examined it. No food or water – it contained paperbacks, with pages yellowed by age and crinkled by cold and moisture. *Of Mice and Men* by John Steinbeck and an omnibus edition of Douglas Adams's *Hitchhikers Guide to the Galaxy.*

I was beginning to dismount from the car when it lurched, causing me to fall awkwardly on my side. I heaved myself upright, heaving to regain my lost breath. What had moved the-- there it was again! The buried car rocked on its corroded suspension and I heard a muffled moan from within. There was no sense in calling "who's there?" since the snow over the doors indicated they'd not been opened for months and I must have inadvertently woken its dead occupant. There came a bellow of rage, accompanied by a thud and another lurch. As the shaking continued, snow slid from its windscreen and I began to move as quickly as I could down the road away from it, rubbing at my aching hip where I'd fallen. The paint can was too awkward and it rattled conspicuously, so I detached it from my belt and cradled it in my arms. Looking over my shoulder, I saw the glass of the windscreen give way, opening up a widening black void in the snow covering. Flailing hands with desiccated, grey fingers appeared. The dead were not fast on their feet, especially not if they'd been motionless in a small, icy hole for some time, but damn, were they relentless when they smelled food. Something in a stained and dishevelled business suit was awkwardly trying to heave its brittle bulk out through the hole, shielding its face from the fading light. I ran for a few paces, trying to increase the distance between us, but my hip must have been mightily bruised and I could not maintain the speed due to the pain. A wail of frustrated rage carried on the breeze from behind me and I shuddered involuntarily as another moan sounded in the far distance in response.

I joined the muddy, ploughed-up slush of the highway, scanning the distance for any signposts, hoping there might be a turn-off to a small village nearby which I didn't previously know about. There were none. A lamp post had corroded through at its base and fallen across the road, presumably in the last few days, but nobody had yet tried to move it. That didn't bode well. Regardless, I knew that I'd be safer in the relative open of a wide road than travelling a narrower one with hedges and walls on all sides.

The featureless sky darkened further; I know from this, as my only scale by which to measure time, that my passage along the highway must have taken something around to half an hour before I came upon a potentially safe-looking shelter and by this time my legs felt like they were made of molten lead. I had lost sight of my pursuer but I knew he was still there, somewhere behind me, obscured by the curve of the road. I would hear occasional grunts, barks and crashes as he slipped and stumbled and, less frequently, his sounds would be echoed by others of his kind as they woke from their slumber.

I would very easily have missed the squat, pitted concrete building, had it not been for the sound of a small, puttering diesel generator from somewhere behind some spindly remnants of trees. I forced my way through the branches and half climbed, half slid down an embankment of compacted snow and ice to the bunker-like structure with its thick and forbidding metal doors - they would need painting white, I mused, but not now. I hammered upon them, calling to whoever might be inside but receiving no reply. After producing enough noise to certainly wake the dead if they weren't already up, I began trying the locks; since corpses are far from skilled at working such devices, a sturdy bolt is usually adequate for keeping them out, although I would usually find myself worrying *what if there happens to be a freakishly intelligent one out there somewhere?* One of the doors into this building had an old fashioned mortis-type lock and swung inward, albeit grudgingly, when the handle was depressed. I wandered gingerly through into the dim interior and was immediately startled by the humidity of the air inside. How long had I been away from warmth? There certainly couldn't be any undead hiding in here, as the stench of decay would be overpowering. Metal stairs led down into the ground and hissing pipes were suspended all over the place. After a short climb down towards another metal door, I found myself in a low-ceilinged room, devoid of any other human life but inhabited by some creatures I'd only ever seen before in photographs: snakes, four of them, all as thick as a grown man's thigh, bright red and, I would guess, at least twice as long as I was tall if they weren't coiled up inside brightly lit glass cases, raised from the floor by metal pedestals. An unfamiliar animal smell hung in the air but I assumed this was not the snakes themselves, if they were cold reptiles? Perhaps it was their food. The beasts seemed to be contentedly asleep beneath bright, hot lightbulbs and my thoughts of wonder turned to those of comfort, as I set the paint can down, undid the webbing on my pack and lowered my aching limbs into a heap in one corner of the room. A snake stirred in its glass enclosure and swung its head around in my direction, forked tongue flicking a few times before it grew bored and returned to its spiralling heap of red scaled bulk.

To have taken the weight off of my feet was heavenly. Would I be able to spend the night here? Whoever the owner of this place might be, they would have to be cruel-hearted in the extreme to turn me out again now, with the sun very nearly set. I removed my worn and ragged boots, splashed a little water from my canteen onto my blistered feet. There was a thud and rattling from the top of the stairs. Was it the resident of this bunker or the dead man pursuing me? The rattling continued, clumsily as dead synapses in dead lobes tried to recall the distant knowledge of how a door handle turns. A dry and crumbling throat mumbled incomprehensibly in protest and I allowed myself to relax a little. I would see another dawn.

About the Author

Warren Hargodd was born in London in 1979. He studied art at the BRIT School of Performing Arts & Technology and then the Colchester Institute, and spent a few months living in Berlin, but otherwise his home has always been England's capital.

He has shambled his way through a long and uninteresting employment history, as well as working freelance as an illustrator of books and magazines by night, and dabbling in writing, animation and music in his (quite limited) spare time. *The Nursery* was his first full-length novel, self-published in 2008. The short stories *Night* and *Kradditho* were written during his work on this project, as a temporary diversions to alleviate writer’s block.

The story of *Subculture* was just something else he’d intended to write.

www.ingramcontent.com/pod-product-compliance
Ingram Content Group UK Ltd.
Pitfield, Milton Keynes, MK11 3LW, UK
UKHW041941190726
13854UKWH00004B/1724